The Collins Book of Stories
for Seven-Year-Olds

The Collins Book of Stories for Seven-Year-Olds

Collected by Julia Eccleshare

Illustrated by Jacqui Thomas

Young Lions
An Imprint of HarperCollins*Publishers*

First published in Great Britain by
HarperCollins in Young Lions 1992

Young Lions is an imprint of the Children's Division,
part of HarperCollins Publishers Ltd,
77–85 Fulham Palace Road,
Hammersmith, London W6 8JB

ISBN 0 00 674046 4

A CIP record for this book is available
from the British Library

This book is set in Ehrhardt

Printed and bound in Great Britain by
Hartnolls Ltd, Bodmin, Cornwall

Contents

Cheese, Peas and Chocolate Pudding

Betty Van Witsen

There was once a little boy who ate cheese, peas and chocolate pudding. Cheese, peas and chocolate pudding. Cheese, peas and chocolate pudding. Every day the same old things: cheese, peas and chocolate pudding.

For breakfast he would have some cheese. Any kind. Cream cheese, American cheese, Swiss cheese, Dutch cheese, Italian cheese, blue cheese, green cheese, yellow cheese, brick cheese. Just cheese for breakfast.

For lunch he ate peas. Green or yellow peas. Frozen peas, canned peas, dried peas, split peas, black-eyed peas. No potatoes, though – just peas for lunch.

And for supper he would have cheese and peas. And chocolate pudding. Cheese, peas and chocolate pudding. Cheese, peas and chocolate pudding. Every day the same old things: cheese, peas and chocolate pudding.

Once his mother bought a lamb chop for him. She cooked it in a little frying pan on the stove, and she put some salt on it, and gave it to the little boy on a blue dish. The boy looked at it. He smelt it. (It did smell delicious!) He even touched it. But . . .

"Is this cheese?" he asked.

"It's a lamb chop, darling," said his mother.

The boy shook his head. "Cheese!" he said. So his mother ate the lamb chop herself, and the boy had some cottage cheese.

One day his big brother was chewing a raw carrot. It sounded so good, the little boy reached his hand out for a bite.

"Sure!" said his brother. "Here!" The little boy *almost* put the carrot in his mouth, but at the last minute he remembered, and he said, "Is this peas?"

"No, it's a carrot," said his brother.

"Peas," said the little boy firmly, handing the carrot back.

Once his father was eating a big dish of raspberry jelly. It looked so shiny and red and cool, the little boy came over and held his mouth open.

"Want a taste?" asked his dad. The little boy looked and looked at the jelly. He almost looked it off the dish. But: "Is it chocolate pudding?" he asked.

"No, son, it's jelly," said his father.

So the little boy frowned and backed away. "Chocolate pudding!" he said.

His grandmother made biscuits for him. "Nope!" said the boy.

His grandfather bought him an ice-cream cone. The little boy just shook his head.

His aunt and uncle invited him for a

fried-chicken dinner. Everybody ate fried chicken and more fried chicken. Except the little boy. And you know what he ate.

Cheese, peas and chocolate pudding. Cheese, peas and chocolate pudding. Every day the same old things: cheese, peas and chocolate pudding.

But one day – ah, one day, a very funny thing happened. The little boy was playing puppy. He lay on the floor and growled and barked and rolled over. He crept to the table where his big brother was having lunch.

"Arf-arf!" he barked.

"Good dog!" said his brother, patting his head. The little boy lay down on his back on the floor and barked again.

But at that minute, his big brother dropped a piece of *something* from his plate. And the little boy's mouth was just about to say "Arf!" And what do you think happened?

Something dropped into the little boy's mouth. He sat up in surprise. Because *something* was on his tongue. And *something* was warm and juicy and delicious!

10

And it didn't taste like cheese. And it did *not* taste like peas. And it certainly wasn't chocolate pudding.

The little boy chewed slowly. Each chew tasted better than the last. He swallowed *something* and opened his mouth again. Wide. As wide as he could.

"Want some more?" asked his brother.

The little boy closed his mouth and thought. "That's not cheese," he said.

"No, it's not," said his brother.

"And it isn't peas."

"No, not peas," said his brother.

"And it couldn't be chocolate pudding."

"No, it certainly is not chocolate pudding," smiled his brother. "It's hamburger."

The little boy thought hard. "I like hamburger," he said.

So his big brother shared the rest of his hamburger with the little boy, and ever after that, guess what!

Ever after that, the little boy ate cheese, peas, and chocolate pudding and hamburger.

Until he was your age, of course. When he was your age, he ate everything.

The Great Mushroom Mistake

Penelope Lively

Birthday presents for mothers can be a problem. In the first place there is the expense. Obviously diamond necklaces and holidays in Bermuda are out of the question, even if your mother is the sort of person who would fancy such things. In the second place there is the difficult matter of choice. A present should be just what the person wants; to know what this might be you have to make a study of the person in question.

Sue and Alan Hancock had studied their

mother as much as most children. That is to say, they knew warning signs of ill temper (a generally frowsty appearance, a tendency to say no in reply to any request) and signs of a good mood when almost anything might be allowed (humming while making the beds, preparation of large meals). And they could hardly help knowing what she was interested in.

Mrs Hancock was good at growing things. The Hancocks' garden did not just bloom: it crackled and exploded and positively burst out with leaf and petal. Mrs Hancock had green fingers, to put it simply. Everything she planted came popping out of the ground and then shot outwards and upwards; her roses and her peas were the envy of the neighbourhood. Whenever she had a spare minute she was out in the garden. Indeed, when the children were small they had been vaguely under the impression that their mother could not stand up straight, because their most usual view of her was of someone bent double like a clothes-peg, peering down at her seedling plants, or scraping and scratching at the soil.

And so birthday presents were not really a problem. There were new trowels and new gardening gloves and special plants and hanks of new twine. But this year they wanted something special – something different, something no one else's mother had. They searched the usual shops, and were not satisfied. Indeed, it was not until the very day before the birthday that they walked past the greengrocer on the corner near their school and saw the very thing.

Outside the shop were two shallow wooden boxes from which bubbled a profusion of gleaming white mushrooms: crisp fresh delicious-looking mushrooms. And alongside the boxes was a notice: GROW YOUR OWN MUSHROOMS! A NEW CROP EVERY DAY!

They looked at each other. Their mother had grown just about everything in her time, but never mushrooms. They went into the shop. They bought a small plastic bag labelled MUSHROOM SPORE, another bag of earthy stuff in which you were supposed to plant it, and an instruction leaflet.

Mrs Hancock was thrilled. She couldn't wait to get going. The instruction leaflet said that the mushrooms liked to grow indoors in a darkish place. A cellar would do nicely, it said, or the cupboard under the stairs. The Hancocks had no cellar and the cupboard under the stairs was full of the sort of thing that takes refuge in cupboards under the stairs: old shoes and suitcases and a broken tennis racket and a chair with only three legs. Mrs Hancock decided that the only place was the cupboard in the spare room, which was used by guests only – and no guest was threatening for some while. The children helped her to spread the earthy stuff out in boxes and scatter the spore. Then, apparently, all they had to do was wait.

During the night, Alan woke once and thought he heard a faint creaking sound, like a tree straining in the wind. And when, in the morning, they opened the door of the spare room cupboard there in the

16

boxes was a fine growth of mushrooms – fat adult mushrooms and baby mushrooms pushing up under and around them. Mrs Hancock was delighted; the children preened themselves on the success of their present; everyone had fried mushrooms for breakfast.

The next day they found the cupboard door half open and mushrooms tumbling out onto the floor. "Gracious!" said Mrs Hancock. "It'll be mushroom soup for lunch today." The instruction leaflet said DO NOT SOW MORE SPORE TILL CROPPING CEASES, so they decided to wait and see what happened. The next day there were as many mushrooms again. They had mushrooms for every meal.

On the third day there were not only mushrooms bursting from the cupboard but a small clutch under the washbasin. There were far too many to eat; Mrs Hancock gave some to the postman and the milkman and the people next door.

That night, the creaking was more definite. Both children heard it; a sound something between a rustling and a splitting – the sound of growth. And in the morning there were mushrooms all over the spare room floor, a clump on the stairs and several clusters under the table in the hall. The Hancocks gazed at them in astonishment. "They *are* doing well," said Mrs Hancock, with a slight trace of anxiety in her voice. It took some time to collect them all up, and the people next door said thanks very much but they couldn't really do with any more. The children were getting heartily tired of mushroom soup. In the end they had to throw a lot away.

Over the next few days, the mushroom invasion continued. They found mushrooms in the bathroom and beside the cooker and in the toy chest. When they got up in the mornings they had to walk downstairs on a carpet of small mushrooms which squeaked faintly underfoot, like colonies of mice. It was when Mrs Hancock had to vacuum mushrooms from the sitting-room carpet that they realized the situation had got quite out of control. "Stop planting the things," said Mr Hancock. "I have," wailed

Mrs Hancock. "I only ever did plant them the once. They just keep coming." "Green fingers," said her husband sourly. "That's the trouble." Everyone looked despairingly at Mrs Hancock's hands: perfectly ordinary sensible-looking hands but clearly, in this instance, fatal.

They filled the dustbins with mushrooms. They took plastic sacks of mushrooms to the town dump. And still they came, bubbling up every night, springing cheerfully from window ledges and skirting-boards and behind pictures. The house smelled of mushroom: a clean, earthy smell.

Mrs Hancock called in the Pest Control Service, a business-like man with a van who took one look at the mushrooms and shook his head in perplexity. "I've never seen anything like it," he said. "Now if it was rats or cockroaches I'd know where I was. Or wasps. Or ants. This is phenomenal." He looked out of the window at the garden, and then at Mrs Hancock; "I'd say you had a way with nature, madam. Ever thought of going into the wholesale business?" He left a can of weedkiller and said he would come back in a few days. Mrs Hancock mopped the whole house out with weedkiller. The next morning, the night's growth of mushrooms looked a little sickly, like someone who has had a late night and a touch of indigestion, but the day after they were as thriving as ever, coming up here, there and everywhere so that the floors of every room looked softly cobbled. The children were sent out to buy yet more black plastic sacks.

The Pest Control man shook his head again. "They've got a hold," he said. "That's what. Frankly, I don't know what to suggest. It's interesting, mind. I wouldn't let the papers get onto it – you could find yourself on the front page." The Hancocks stared at him coldly. "I'll have a think," he said, going out of the front door. "The great thing is, don't panic."

That evening, Mrs Hancock said, "There's nothing for it. We're going to have to call in Aunt Sadie." There was a silence; Mr Hancock sighed. "A desperate measure," he said. "But I see your point."

Many families have an Aunt Sadie: an expert all-purpose undefeatable long-distance interferer. The relation who scents defects as soon as she has one foot inside the door – "Pity that paint turned out the wrong colour", "I see Sue's hair's still growing dead straight", "I'm wondering if Alan's teeth don't need a brace". Aunt Sadie could kill any occasion stone dead: Christmas, birthdays, family outings. Strong men fled at the sight of Aunt Sadie. And there was nothing Aunt Sadie enjoyed more than muscling in on a situation (preferably uninvited) and, as she called it 'lending a willing hand'. What chance, Mr Hancock agreed, would a few mushrooms have against Aunt Sadie?

Aunt Sadie, dropping her suitcase in the hall, stalked through the house inspecting. She peered at the mushrooms and the mushrooms, just starting on their second crop of the day, peeped back from cracks in the floorboards and sidled out from under the carpets. She fetched the dustpan and shovelled out a couple of pounds of them

from inside the grandfather clock, where they had been surging up unnoticed for several days. The Hancocks watched with interest. Aunt Sadie, in her time, had reduced a six foot traffic warden to tears and disrupted an entire police station. She went upstairs and could be heard tramping around. When she came down Mr Hancock said, "Well, Sadie – bit out of your line, eh?" This, of course, was meant to provoke, and it did.

Aunt Sadie glared at him. "I'll want a free hand. I'll want everyone out of the way except the children. You'd better take Mary for a short holiday."

"But I don't want a holiday . . ." Mrs Hancock began.

"You'll have to. There's no two ways about it. It's having you here that's encouraged the things. I always said all that gardening was unnatural." She rolled up her sleeves.

"What do you want *us* for?" asked Sue.

"Labour force," snapped Aunt Sadie.

The next few days were pandemonium.

23

"There's nothing," said Aunt Sadie decisively, "that a good spring-clean won't deal with." Carpets, curtains, chairs and tables were hurled hither and thither. The house looked as though a bomb had hit it. The children scurried to and fro with buckets and scrubbing-brushes.

The mushrooms grew, undaunted.

The children were sent shopping. "Ten gallons of disinfectant!" said the manager of the hardware shop. "Jeyes Fluid *and* ammonia *and* a quart of insecticide! You people in some kind of trouble?"

Aunt Sadie, with the children panting behind her, scrubbed and sprayed and swabbed. For five days she and the mushrooms did battle. A dose of Jeyes Fluid had them coming up blackened but valiantly fighting back. Insecticide and flea powder sent them reeling for a couple of days. "We've got them on the run!" said Aunt Sadie grimly, but then a new wave broke out from the airing cupboard. The war was on again.

All this had quite distracted Aunt Sadie

from her usual occupation when visiting: general interference. In the normal way of things she would have been busy suggesting that everything the family did should be done differently and in particular that the children were a total disaster in terms of appearance, behaviour and anything else you like to mention. Their health, especially, was of intense interest: they were spotty, she would announce, or pasty-looking, or too large or too small or too fat or too thin, and various appalling tonics and potions were produced to set matters right.

With relief, Sue and Alan realized that on this occasion she was far too taken up with the mushrooms to pay them much attention at all. Until one evening Alan made the mistake of coughing.

"You've got a cough," said Aunt Sadie, instantly alert.

"Bit of biscuit got stuck," said Alan hastily.

"I know a chronic cough when I hear one," said Aunt Sadie, grim. She reached into the enormous handbag that accompanied her even into the bathroom. Out came a bottle of fearsome-looking brown stuff, and a spoon. "Open your mouth."

Whether what happened next was an accident or not will never be known. As the first horrific whiff of the cough mixture reached Alan's nose he gave a kind of convulsive snort. The cough mixture blew from the spoon, the spoon flew from Aunt Sadie's hand, Aunt Sadie with a cry of annoyance leaned forward to rescue it and knocked over the open bottle upon the table, which lurched to the floor gushing thick brown cough mixture in all directions. Everyone began to blame everyone else until suddenly Sue cried, "Look!"

The advancing tide of cough mixture had reached a clump of mushrooms that had sprung up unnoticed from the skirtingboard. And as it did so a very curious thing happened. The mushrooms vanished. They simply expired. One moment they were there and the next there was nothing but a little heap of dust and a puddle of cough mixture.

"Well!" said Aunt Sadie, staring, "That's interesting . . . "

"If it does that to people too," said Alan, "it's a jolly good thing I didn't swallow it."

Aunt Sadie ignored him, "I think," she said thoughtfully, "we may be on to something."

This time Aunt Sadie did the shopping herself. It is not just anyone who can persuade a chemist to make up several gallons of cough mixture, and supply it in a large can with a spray attachment. What the chemist said or thought is not known; Aunt Sadie had a way of discouraging unwelcome curiosity. Anyway, she returned, armed with the new weapon, and set to work. And within a matter of hours there was not a mushroom in sight, nor did any appear the next morning, nor the next. Aunt Sadie stalked around the house in triumph, and sent for Mr and Mrs Hancock. The children, eyeing the remains of the cough mixture with awe, were quite extraordinarily careful not to cough.

And that was the end of the great mushroom mistake. For her next birthday the children gave their mother six handkerchiefs and some talcum powder, an unadventurous present but a safe one. And Aunt Sadie's reputation soared to even greater heights; there was nothing, it was generally agreed, with which she could not deal. The government, Mr Hancock suggested, would do well to hire her and keep her in hand for use in case of riots, epidemics, earthquake or flood. And the Pest Control man, who happened to call back the day before Aunt Sadie left, is still trying to get the recipe for that cough mixture from her.

Vasilissa, Baba Yaga, and the Little Doll

Retold by Naomi Lewis

In a far-off land in a far-off time, on the edge of a great forest, lived a girl named Vasilissa. Ah, poor Vasilissa! She was no more than eight years old when her mother died. But she had a friend, and that one was better than most. Who was this friend? A doll. As the mother lay ill she had called the child to her bedside. "Vasilissa," she said, "here is a little doll. Take good care of her, and whenever you are in great need, give her some food and ask for her help; she will tell

29

you what to do. Take her, with my blessing; but remember, she is your secret; no one else must know of her at all. Now I can die content."

The father of Vasilissa grieved for a time, then married a new wife, thinking that she would care for the little girl. But did she indeed! She had two daughters of her own, and not one of the three had a grain of love for Vasilissa. From early dawn to the last light of day, in the hot sun or the icy wind, they kept her toiling at all the hardest tasks, in or out of the house; never did she have a word of thanks. Yet whatever they set her to do was done, and done in time. For when she truly needed help she would set her doll on a ledge or table, give her a little food and drink, and tell the doll her troubles. With her help all was done.

One day in the late autumn the father had to leave for the town, a journey of many days. He set off at earliest dawn.

Darkness fell early. Rain beat on the cottage windows; the wind howled down the chimney – just the time for the wife to work a plan she had in mind. To each of the girls she gave a task: the first was set to making lace, the second to knitting stockings, Vasilissa to spinning.

"No stirring from your place, my girls, before you have done," said the woman. Then, leaving them a single candle, she went to bed.

The three worked on for a while, but the light was small, and flickered. One sister pretended to trim the wick and it went out altogether – just as the mother had planned.

"Now we're in trouble," said the girl. "For where's the new light to come from?"

"There's only one place," said her sister, "and that's from Baba Yaga."

"That's right," said the other. "But who's to go?

*My needles shine;
The job's not mine.*"

"I can manage too," said the other.

*My lace-pins shine;
the job's not mine.*

31

Vasilissa must go."

"Yes, Vasilissa must go!" they cried together. And they pushed her out of the door.

Now who was Baba Yaga? She was a mighty witch; her hut was set on claws, like the legs of giant hens. She rode in a mortar over the highest mountains, speeding it on with the pestle, sweeping away her traces with a broom. And she would crunch up in a trice any human who crossed her path.

But Vasilissa had a friend, and that one better than most. She took the doll from her pocket, and set some bread before her. "Little doll," she said, "they are sending me into the forest to fetch a light from Baba Yaga's hut – and who has ever returned from there? Help me, little doll."

The doll ate, and her eyes grew bright as stars. "Have no fear," said she. "While I am with you nothing can do you harm. But remember – no one else must know of your secret. Now let us start."

How dark it was in the forest of towering trees! How the leaves hissed, how the branches creaked and moaned in the wind! But Vasilissa walked resolutely on, hour after hour. Suddenly, the earth began to tremble and a horseman thundered by. Both horse and rider were glittering white, hair and mane, swirling cloak and bridle too; and as they passed, the sky showed the first white light of dawn.

Vasilissa journeyed on, then again she heard a thundering noise, and a second horse and rider flashed into sight. Both shone red as scarlet, red as flame, swirling cloak and bridle too; as they rode beyond her view, the sun rose high. It was day.

On she walked, on and on, until she reached a clearing in the woods. In the centre was a hut – but the hut had feet; and they were the claws of hens. It was Baba Yaga's home, no doubt about that. All around was a fence of bones, and the posts were topped with skulls: a fearful sight in the fading light! And as she gazed, a third horseman thundered past; but this time horse and rider were black and black, swirling cloak and bridle

33

too. They vanished into the gloom, and it was night. But, as darkness fell, the eyes of the skulls lit up like lamps and everything in the glade could be seen as sharp as day.

Swish! Swoosh! Varoom! Varoom! As Vasilissa stood there, frozen stiff with fear, a terrible noise came from over the forest. The wind screeched, the leaves hissed – Baba Yaga was riding home in her huge mortar, using her pestle as an oar, sweeping away the traces with her broom. At the gate of the hut she stopped, and sniffed the air with her long nose.

"Phoo! Phoo! I smell Russian flesh!" she croaked. "Who's there? Out you come!"

Vasilissa took courage, stepped forward and made a low curtsey.

"It is I, Vasilissa. My sisters sent me for a light, since ours went out."

"Oh, so that's it!" said the witch. "I know those girls, and their mother too. Well, nothing's for nothing, as they say; you must work for me for a while, then we'll see about the light." She turned

to the hut and sang in a high shrill screech:

> *"Open gates! Open gates!*
> *Baba Yaga waits."*

The weird fence opened; the witch seized the girl's arm in her bony fingers and pushed her into the hut. "Now," she said, "get a light from the lamps outside," – she meant the skulls – "and serve my supper. It's in the oven, and the soup's in the cauldron there." She lay down on a bench while Vasilissa carried the food to the table until she was quite worn out, but she dared not stop. And the witch devoured much more than ten strong men could have eaten – whole geese and hens and roasted pigs; loaf after loaf; huge buckets of beer and wine, cider and Russian kvass. At last, all that remained was a crust of bread.

"There's your supper, girl," said the witch. "But you must earn it, mind; I don't like greed. While I'm off tomorrow you must clear out the yard; it hasn't been touched for years, and it quite blocks out the view. Then you must sweep the hut, wash the linen, cook the dinner – and mind you cook enough; I was half-starved tonight. Then – for I'll have no lazybones around – there's another little job. You see that sack? It's full of black beans, wheat and poppy seed, some other things too, I dare say. Sort them out into their separate lots, and if a single one is out of place, woe betide! Into the cauldron you shall go, and I'll crunch you up for breakfast in a trice."

So saying, she lay down by the stove and was instantly fast asleep. Sno-o-o-re . . . Sno-o-o-re . . . It was a horrible sound.

Vasilissa took the doll from her pocket and gave her the piece of bread. "Little doll," said she. "How am I to do all these tasks? Or even one of them? How can a little doll like you help now? We are lost indeed."

"Vasilissa," said the doll. "Again I tell you, have no fear. Say your prayers and go to sleep. Tomorrow knows what is hidden from yesterday."

She slept – but she woke early, before the first glimmer of day. Where should she start on the mountain of work? Then she heard a thundering of hoofs; white horse and white rider flashed past the window – suddenly it was dawn. The light in the skulls' eyes dwindled and went out. Then the poor girl hid in the shadows, for she saw Baba Yaga get to her feet – Creak! Creak! – and shuffle to the door. There, the witch gave a piercing whistle, and mortar, pestle and broom came hurtling towards her, stopping where she stood. In she stepped, off she rode, over tree-tops, through the clouds, using the pestle like an oar, sweeping away her traces with the broom. Just as she soared away, the red horse and red rider thundered past: suddenly it was day, and the sun shone down.

Vasilissa turned away from the window, but what was this? She could not believe her eyes.

Every task was done. The yard was cleared, the linen washed, the grains and the seeds were all in separate bins, the dinner was set to cook. And there was the little doll, waiting to get back in her pocket.

"All you need to do," said the doll, "is to lay the table and serve it all, hot and hot, when she returns. But keep your wits about you all the same, for she's a sly one."

The winter daylight faded fast; again there was a thundering of hoofs; black horse, black rider sped through the glade and were gone. Darkness fell, and the eyes of the skulls once more began to glow. And then, with a swish and a roar, down swept the mortar, out stepped Baba Yaga.

"Well, girl, why are you standing idle? You know what I told you."

"The work is all done, Baba Yaga."

Baba Yaga looked and looked, but done it all was. So she sat down, grumbling and mumbling, to eat her supper. It was good, very good: it put her in a pleasant humour, for a witch.

"Tell me, girl, why do you sit there as if you were dumb?"

"Baba Yaga, I did not dare to speak – but, now, if you permit it, may I ask a question?"

"Ask if you will, but remember that not

every question leads to good. The more you know, the older you grow."

"Well, Baba Yaga, can you tell me, who is the white rider on the white horse, the one who passed at dawn?"

"He is my Bright Morning, and he brings the earliest light."

"Then who is the rider all in red on the flame-red horse?"

"Ah, he is my Fiery Sun and brings the day."

"And who is the horseman all in black on the coal-black horse?"

"He is my Dark Night. All are my faithful servants. Now I shall ask *you* a question; mind you answer me properly. How did you do all those tasks I set you?"

Vasilissa recalled her mother's words, never to tell the secret of the doll.

"My mother gave me a blessing before she died, and that helps me when in need."

"A blessing! I want no blessed children here! Out you get! Away! Away!" And she pushed her through the door. "You've earned your pay – now take it." She took down one of the gate-post skulls, fixed it on a stick, and thrust it into Vasilissa's hand. "Now – off !"

Vasilissa needed no second bidding. She hastened on, her path now lit by the eyes of the fearful lamp. And so, at last, she was home.

"Why have you taken so long?" screamed the mother and the sisters. They had been in darkness ever since she left. They had gone in every direction to borrow a light, but once it was inside in the house, every flame went out. So they seized the skull with joy.

But the glaring eyes stared back; wherever they turned they could not escape the scorching rays. Soon, all that remained of the three was a little ash. Then the light of the skull went out for ever; its task was done.

Vasilissa buried it in the garden, and a bush of red roses sprang up on the spot. She did not fear to be alone, for the little doll kept her company. And when her father returned, rejoicing to see her, this tale she told him, just as it has been told to you.

The Lory Who Longed for Honey

Leila Berg

Once upon a time, in a hot sunny country, lived a very bright and beautiful parrot. He was red and green and gold and blue, with a dark purple top to his head. His real name was Lory. And he lived on honey.

There were hundreds of flowers growing among the trees, so all he had to do when he was hungry was to fly down and lick the honey out of the flowers. As a matter of fact, he had a tongue that was specially shaped for getting honey out of flowers. So he always had plenty to eat, and managed very well. All day long he flew about in the hot sunshine, while the monkeys chattered and the bright birds screamed. And as long as he had plenty of honey, he was perfectly happy.

Then one day a sailor came to the forest looking for parrots. He found the parrot that liked honey and took him away. He didn't know that this parrot's real name was a Lory. He didn't know that he had a tongue specially shaped for getting honey out of flowers. He didn't even know he liked honey. He only knew he was a very bright and beautiful parrot and he meant to take him to England and sell him. So on board the ship he fed the parrot on sunflower seeds and taught him to say: "What have you got, what have you got, what have you got for me?" And whenever the Lory said this, the sailor gave him a sunflower seed. Although, as a matter of fact, he would very much sooner have had honey.

When they reached England, the sailor sold the parrot who liked honey to an old lady who lived in a cottage on a hill. She didn't know much about parrots. She didn't know the parrot was a Lory. She didn't know he had a special tongue for licking honey out of flowers. She didn't even know he liked honey.

But she thought his red and green feathers, his gold and blue feathers, and the dark purple feathers on the top of his head were beautiful. She called him Polly, and fed him on bits of bread and biscuit.

Whenever he said, as he often did: "What have you got, what have you got, what have you got for me?" she would give him a bit of bread or biscuit. But, of course, he would very much sooner have had honey.

Now the old lady lived by herself and had to work very hard to make enough money to buy food. Generally she had just bread and margarine for tea, because she couldn't afford to buy honey even for herself, although she liked it.

Then one day when she wasn't in the least expecting it, the old lady's nephew who lived in South Africa sent her a present. It was a wooden box carefully packed with straw. Some of the straw was already poking between the boards, but it was impossible to tell what was inside.

When the postman brought it, he said: "Looks like a nice surprise, lady. Maybe some jam or some fruit."

She carried the box carefully into her sitting-room and unfastened it. It wasn't jam or fruit. It was six jars of honey all wrapped up in straw. Inside was a note which said:

Dear Auntie,

I have managed to get a very nice job in South Africa, and I am making quite a bit of money. I am sure you are not able to buy all the things you need, so I am sending you six jars of honey. If you like them, I will send some more.

Love from your nephew – Robert

When she had read the letter she was tremendously excited and pleased, because it was so long since anyone had sent her a present and today it wasn't even her birthday. She took out the jars very carefully and put them in a row in the larder. Then she cleared up all the straw and paper and string, and said to herself: "I'll start the first jar at tea-time today."

When the clock struck half past three, the old lady put the kettle on the gas, and began to cut some bread. It was certainly rather early for tea, but the old lady was so excited about the honey that she couldn't wait any longer. She put the bread and margarine on the table, took a plate and a knife, and a cup and saucer and spoon out of the cupboard, and then she went to the larder.

All this made Polly very excited. He wasn't in his cage, but on a separate perch where he could turn somersaults if he liked. The old lady let him sit here in the afternoons. He could tell it was tea-time, and when the old lady went to the larder he expected she would bring out some cake or fruit.

So he shouted at the top of his voice: "What have you got, what have you got, what have you got for me?" When the old lady brought out neither cake nor fruit, but only a jar of yellow stuff, Polly was rather puzzled. But as soon as he saw her take some on her knife and spread the sticky stuff on her bread, and eat it with such pleasure, he knew it was honey.

And as soon as he knew it was honey, he knew he absolutely must think of some way of getting it for himself.

The old lady never dreamt of giving the Lory honey. She didn't know much about parrots. She didn't know he was called a Lory. She didn't know he had a tongue specially shaped for getting honey out of flowers. She didn't even know he liked honey.

But all the time the old lady was spreading the honey on her first slice of bread and thinking how wonderfully kind her nephew was to send it, and what an unexpected treat it was, the Lory was working out a plan.

Now parrots, as you know, are very clever at remembering words and also at imitating people, and sometimes when they talk they can make their voice sound as if it is coming from a different part of the house altogether, so that you have no idea it is the parrot talking at all.

While the old lady was eating her bread and honey and enjoying it tremendously, she suddenly heard a *Miaow!* It was really the Lory, but she didn't know that.

"There's a kitten outside," she said. "Poor thing, I expect it's lost. I'll let it in so that it can get warm by the fire." And she went to the door and opened it.

Polly just had time to flutter on to the table and take a mouthful of honey with his special tongue and get on his perch again before she came back.

"How very strange," she said, "I'm sure I heard a kitten. Yet I've looked in the street, and there isn't a kitten to be seen."

Polly winked and shouted: "What have you got, what have you got, what have you got for me?" But the old lady still didn't know he was after the honey.

While the lady was spreading her *second* slice of bread, he thought of another plan. This time he made a noise like the kettle boiling over.

"Goodness!" cried the old lady, jumping

up. "That will put the stove out, unless I hurry."

And while she rushed out into the kitchen, Polly flew down and took his second big mouthful of honey.

"That's very peculiar," said the old lady, coming back again just as Polly scrambled on to his perch. "The kettle's perfectly all right, and not boiling over at all." But she still didn't understand the Lory was after her honey.

Then he had what he thought was his best plan of all. He made a noise like big drops of rain falling on the roof.

"Oh heavens!" said the poor old lady. "Now I shall have to bring all the washing in."

And she left her tea with the pot of honey standing on the table, and went outside to fetch in the washing before it got soaked.

She was a long time, because she had washed a table-cloth, two sheets, a pillow-slip, a towel, a frock, a cardigan and the curtains from the sitting-room. And while she was taking them all off the line, the

Lory was swallowing honey as fast as he could.

At last, her arms full of washing, the old lady came back into the room. "That's funny," she said, as she looked at the window. "The sun is shining as brightly as ever. I do believe I've brought all the washing in for nothing."

"And that's funnier still!" she went on with a little scream, looking at the table. "I do believe someone's been eating my honey!"

She picked up the jar and looked at it. There was just a scraping left at the bottom. Yet she had only opened the jar a few minutes ago.

"It must be a burglar," she said, and feeling very brave she began to look under the furniture and inside the cupboards and wherever a burglar might find space to hide.

All the time she was hunting, the Lory was turning somersaults on his perch and shrieking at the top of his voice: "What have you got, what have you got, what have you got for me?" He felt very pleased with himself, and he didn't care a bit that he had made the old lady go to all the trouble of bringing in her washing, and on top of that had eaten almost the whole of a jar of honey that her nephew had sent from South Africa.

When the old lady had decided there was no burglar in the house, she went back to the tea-table. And then she noticed drips of honey leading over the table-cloth, over the floor, and up to Polly's perch. She reached up and touched his perch, and, sure enough, that was sticky too.

"Why, you rascal!" she said. "I do believe it was you who stole the honey."

And that was how the old lady who didn't know much about parrots discovered that Lories like honey better than anything else in the world. After that, she always gave her Lory some honey for his tea, and she managed it quite well because her nephew in South Africa sent her six jars every month.

But do you know, she never found out it was the Lory who played those tricks on her just to get a taste of her honey!

How Fire Came to Earth

Grace Hallworth

At the beginning of time, long before man
was formed, there was no fire on earth.
Everywhere was cold and bleak and a
grey mist shrouded land and sea. Woolly-
coated creatures huddled together in caves
and feathered ones clustered wherever they
could find shelter. Some creatures made
their homes in the ground, while a few
burrowed to the very depths of the earth
and were never seen again.

High above earth the great Sunbird

basked in the glow of a fire that burned day and night. He did not know of the suffering of earth creatures. His home was too far away. At last the creatures could bear the cold no longer so they held a meeting.

When all were gathered Leopard began: "Two of my litter are dead from cold."

At this point Seagull interrupted: "It is hard to find enough shelter to keep our nests warm."

Every living creature complained about the cold. Only Owl kept silent.

When all had spoken she said: "Mighty Thunderbird shoots fire-sticks across the sky when he is angry. Let us ask him for some of his fire."

They chose Eagle to seek him out for he could fly higher than any other creature. Besides, Eagle knew where to find him. He flew to a mountain in the middle of the ocean where Thunderbird rested after his noisy outbursts. There he waited for many days. When Thunderbird arrived, Eagle approached him and said: "Great one who makes thunder-fire, I come from earth where many creatures die from cold. Will you give some of your fire to warm earth?"

"My fire is for the sky," replied Thunderbird. "You could not use it on earth, but my brother has a fire tree. I will ask him to give you a branch from it."

And he went at once to Sunbird and said: "Brother, the wretched creatures on earth perish because of cold. Give them fire so that they may live!"

But Sunbird said: "No, I will not give them fire. Their knowledge is not sufficient to guard it and they will destroy earth."

Again and again Thunderbird pleaded for the earth creatures but Sunbird would not yield.

One night when his brother was asleep, Thunderbird stole a branch from the fire tree. He fitted it to his bow and shot it down on to the mountain where he had met Eagle. It went straight to the heart of a dead sycamore tree and set it alight. Earth creatures saw the blazing mountain and were anxious to get hold of fire, but

Eagle was away and no one knew when he would return. One of them would have to cross the water to get to the blazing mountain before fire died away.

"Whooooo? W-hoohoo-hooo? Whoo will fly to get fire?" called Owl.

"I will. I will. I will fly to the mountain and bring back fire," said a bird with beautiful silver-grey feathers. And off she flew across the sea. She had never flown so far or so high. She was buffeted by strong winds but held her course and flew steadily on.

On the mountain red-hot flames leapt and crackled and the bird could find no place to alight. She would have to seize a fire-stick and return at once. Round and round she flew looking for an opening but as she drew near fire, a change came over her. She felt a tingling, prickling sensation. Grey-black wisps curled and twisted around her eyes and snaked into her mouth. She tried to escape by flying high above them and the cool clean air cleared her eyes and helped her to breathe.

In her breast, the bird felt that she must

soon leave, for the struggle with fire had tired her. Cautiously she dropped to a lower air stream just above fire, where the wisps were small and weak. Once more sharp pains shot through her body and as the stabbing pains increased, her feathers began to fall off. "Haaargh! Haaargh! Haaargh!" Her harsh cries of pain and fear came from a throat sore from heat and smoke. Her wings were badly burnt and the skin on her feet hung like strips of yellow ribbon. She mustered all her strength and lifted herself up and away. She was fortunate that the wind was blowing in the direction of the Homeland. She flew low, and the spray from the waves soothed her aching body.

At the water's edge, the creatures were waiting for the bird to return with fire. Instead, they saw a bedraggled creature with eyes as red as fire itself. Her silvery feathers were blackened. And they have remained that way to this day, for she had become the bird we now call the Raven.

"Whuu did this to you?" howled Wolf.

"It was fire himself. He stabs you with

sharp points while his wisps force your eyes shut and squeeze breath from your body. We cannot tame fire," said the bird.

"I can. No one is swifter than I. I will, I will, I will go to the mountain and seize fire," boasted Leopard. Immediately he dived into the sea and started to swim across the wide expanse of cold water. Waves as tall as Leopard tossed him about. Swift treacherous currents tried to pull him under but his strokes were powerful.

On the mountain the fire blazed.

Leopard decided to swim around and see where he could best attack fire. He found a winding path that led to the top of the mountain. Suddenly he was enveloped in a thick black cloud which began to smother him. His eyes hurt so much that he couldn't see. Frantically he spun round and round, trying to escape, but fire was choking the breath from his body. He was beginning to weaken when he saw a golden light, and he rushed through it. It had a sting fiercer than bees robbed of their honey.

He roared a fearful roar, leapt into the

air and fell headlong into the sea. It was the cold water that saved him, cooling his feet, his body, his face.

Leopard hurt badly all over. His fur was singed and his legs were stiff. Partly floating and partly swimming, he made his way back home. The creatures were so sure that Leopard would bring fire that they had prepared a large pit in the forest which they filled with leaves and dried seaweed.

"We will tame fire and keep him alive here. Then every creature may take some of fire whenever there is need," said Owl.

As they waited at the water's edge for Leopard, they talked of all the things they would do when they had fire.

But what was this?

Could this be graceful Leopard, so fleet of foot?

The creatures could not believe their eyes. Leopard's beautiful golden coat was now threadbare and spotted with black soot. They watched in amazement as he limped away into the forest.

Night, the black curtain, fell, and still fire blazed.

From a distance the earth creatures watched, glad at least for the warmth that came from fire's brightness.

Who dared to fetch fire now that powerful Leopard had failed?

"WhoooOOO? W-hoo-hoo-hoooo? Whooooooo?" Owl's mournful cries echoed through the night.

"Let me! Let me! Let me fly to the mountain," pleaded Bat.

She had been asleep for most of the day. Now she was wide awake.

No one heard Bat's gentle twittering. No one saw the small black creature fly off in the dark. She had no fear of the journey for she was used to travelling long distances, and the thought of bringing back fire spurred her on. As she approached the mountain, she saw fires flare up like rockets, showering sparks everywhere. Bat was spellbound by the bright colours. She flew close, yet felt no pain from fire's light. She darted down to seize a twig of fire and it spat a bunch of sparks right in her eyes. Shrieking, she rose in the air, flying blind, for her eyes were badly burnt.

"Can't see! Can't see! Can't see!" she cried.

"Seeseeseek! Seeseeseek! Seeseeseek!" keened the other bats who heard her cry of distress. Their high-pitched calls helped her to find the way back to the Homeland and the creatures who anxiously waited at the water's edge. All gathered around to see what fire had done to Bat.

"Fire paints bright pictures but when you try to take them he throws dust in your eyes. Fire is cruel," sobbed Bat.

And ever since that night Bat has been blind. She shuns the light of day and lives in dark places.

Snake scolded. "Iss s-s-so small a creature that s-s-sets out to s-s-steal fire! There muss be no more of thisss foolissness. I will s-s-seek fire if Eagle isss not back s-s-soon."

Now Spider was going to tell the other

creatures about her idea to catch fire and bring him back. But when she heard Snake scolding Bat she said nothing. Instead she crawled away to work on her plan. She would build a bridge across the sea to the mountain and fetch fire. She began to weave a pattern which she had practised so often that she could do the movement in her sleep. As she spun, she sang a song:

"In and out and in and out
Up and down and round about
In and out and in and out
Pay the silken thread far out."

Again and again she repeated the movements as she sang. Hour after hour she spun her strong silken thread and paid it out. At last her feet touched ground. She had arrived.

Spider scurried around, looking for something to catch fire. It must be

something flat that would sit on her back
something that would not let water in
something that would not let fire out.

Near the water she found a flat stone, but it could not hold fire in.

Further along the beach she saw a piece of wood. Fire had burnt a hole through it.

Dawn flooded the sky reflecting the colours of fire below.

Spider searched everywhere.

Half-buried in the sand she saw a shell. It was flat enough to sit on her back and hollow enough to keep fire in and water out. Spider carried it to where fire was burning brightest.

Phtt! Phtt! A small piece of burning wood broke off from a branch and flew into the shell. At once Spider placed the shell on her back and set out for the bridge she had woven. When she got there fire had destroyed the silken bridge.

She didn't know what to do. Fire was spreading and soon there would be no place to stand. There was no other way out. She would have to go into the sea.

But Spider couldn't swim!

Then she remembered that whenever she saw the tide coming in at dawn, it flowed gently in to shore. Could she risk going into the sea with fire on her back? She would have to hurry, for already she could see a faint glow of morning light through the night curtain. Quickly she spun a sticky bell-shaped web under her body to keep her afloat. She stepped bravely into the sea.

All morning Spider floated on the gentle tidestream towards Homeland. She was sleepy and tired but dared not sleep for she didn't know when the tide might become choppy and fast. She sang a song to keep her awake:

> *"Rock and sway and rock and sway*
> *Tide-stream flow-in all the way*
> *Rock and sway and rock and sway*
> *Fire safe from briny spray."*

At last the tide washed her up on the shore where she had left the others. All the creatures had gone home! There was no one to greet Spider or to lift the shell off her back. She struggled up the beach and along the path to the pit in the forest.

But now, fire was beginning to burn through the shell and Spider could feel the heat on her back and the hairs of her legs. At last she could bear the pain no more. She tilted fire on the ground and curled up in a tight ball to protect herself. Greedily, fire licked the ground round the frightened creature, ready to devour her. And he would have done so – but Eagle returned just then and saw what was happening. He swooped down, and gripped Spider in his talons and took her away to safety near the forest pool.

And so it was that this tiny creature conquered fire and brought it to the Homeland so that all the earth's creatures might have warmth. Spider knows that fire lurks in the forest waiting for a chance to punish her, so she lives in water where fire cannot reach her. The water spider still carries the splash of colour where fire marked her.

Theseus and the Minotaur

Retold by Charles Kingsley

Long ago there ruled a great king in Athens called Aegeus, and his son, Theseus, was a hero who had done many brave and mighty deeds.

Now the whole country was happy and at peace except for one great sorrow. Minos, King of Crete, had fought against the Athenians and had conquered them; and before returning to Crete he had made a hard and cruel peace. Each year the Athenians were forced to send seven young men and seven maidens to be sacrificed to the Minotaur. This was a monster who lived in the labyrinth, a winding path among rocks and caves. So each spring seven youths and maidens, chosen by lot, journeyed in a ship with black sails to the shores of Crete, to be torn to pieces by the savage Minotaur.

One spring, when the herald from King Minos arrived, Theseus determined to make an end of the beast, and rid his father's people of this horrible evil. He went and told Aegeus that when the black-sailed ship set out on the morrow he would go too and slay the Minotaur.

"But how will you slay him, my son?" said Aegeus. "For you must leave your club and your shield behind, and be cast to the monster, defenceless and naked like the rest."

And Theseus said, "Are there no stones in that labyrinth; and have I not fists and teeth?"

Then Aegeus clung to his knees; but he would not hear; and at last he let him go, weeping bitterly, and said only these words –

"Promise me but this, if you return in peace, though that may hardly be: take down the black sail of the ship (for I shall watch for it all day upon the cliffs), and hoist instead a white sail, that I may know from far off that you are safe."

And Theseus promised, and went out to the market-place where the herald stood, while they drew lots for the youths and maidens who were to sail in that doleful crew. And the people stood wailing and weeping as the lot fell on this one and on that; but Theseus strode into the midst, and cried,

"Here is a youth who needs no lot. I myself will be one of the seven."

And the herald asked in wonder, "Fair youth, know you whither you are going?"

And Theseus said, "I know. Let us go down to the black-sailed ship."

So they went down to the black-sailed ship, seven maidens, and seven youths, and Theseus before them all, and the people following them, lamenting. But Theseus whispered to his companions, "Have hope, for the monster is not immortal." Then their hearts were comforted a little; but they wept as they went on board, and the cliffs of Sunium, and all the isles of the Aegean Sea, rang with the voice of their lamentations as they sailed on towards their deaths in Crete.

And at last they came to Crete, and to Knossus, beneath the peaks of Ida, and to the palace of Minos the great king, to whom Zeus himself taught laws – so he was the wisest of all mortal kings, and conquered all the Aegean isles; and his ships were as many as the seagulls, and his palace was like a marble hill.

But Theseus stood before Minos, and they looked each other in the face. And Minos bade take them to prison, and cast them to the monster one by one. Then Theseus cried,

"A boon, O Minos! Let me be thrown first to the beast. For I came hither for that very purpose, of my own will, and not by lot."

"Who art thou, then, brave youth?"

"I am the son of him whom of all men thou

hatest most, Aegeus, the king of Athens, and I am come here to end this matter."

And Minos pondered awhile, looking steadfastly at him, and he answered at last mildly,

"Go back in peace, my son. It is a pity that one so brave should die."

But Theseus said, "I have sworn that I will not go back till I have seen the monster face to face."

And at that Minos frowned, and said, "Then thou shalt see him; take the madman away."

And they led Theseus away into prison, with the other youths and maidens.

But Ariadne, Minos's daughter, saw him, as she came out of her white stone hall; and she loved him for his courage and his majesty, and said, "Shame that such a youth should die!" And by night she went down to the prison, and told him all her heart, and said,

"Flee down to your ship at once, for I have bribed the guards before the door. Flee, you and all your friends, and go back in peace to Greece; and take me, take me with you! for I dare not stay after you are gone; for my father will kill me miserably, if he knows what I have done."

And Theseus stood silent a while; for he was astonished and confounded by her beauty. But at last he said, "I cannot go home in peace, till I have seen and slain this Minotaur, and avenged the deaths of the youths and maidens, and put an end to the terrors of my land."

"And will you kill the Minotaur? How, then?"

"I know not, nor do I care. But he must be strong if he be too strong for me."

Then she loved him all the more, and said, "But when you have killed him, how will you find your way out of the labyrinth?"

"I know not, neither do I care. But it must be a strange road, if I do not find it out before I have eaten up the monster's carcase."

Then she loved him all the more, and said,

"Fair youth, you are too bold; but I can

help you, weak as I am. I will give you a sword, and with that perhaps you may slay the beast; and a clue of thread, and by that, perhaps, you may find your way out again. Only promise me that if you escape safely you will take me home with you to Greece; for my father will surely kill me, if he knows what I have done."

Then Theseus laughed and said, "Am I not safe enough now?" And he hid the sword in his bosom, and rolled up the clue in his hand; and then he swore to Ariadne, and fell down before her and kissed her hands and her feet; and she wept over him a long while, and then went away; and Theseus lay down and slept sweetly. When the evening came, the guards arrived and led him away to the labyrinth.

And he went down into that doleful gulf, through winding paths among the rocks, under caverns, and arches, and galleries, and over heaps of fallen stone. And he turned on the left hand, and on the right hand, and went up and down, till his head was dizzy; but all the while he held his clue.

For when he went in he had fastened it to a stone, and left it to unroll out of his hand as he went on; and it lasted him till he met the Minotaur, in a narrow chasm between black cliffs.

And when he saw him he stopped a while, for he had never seen so strange a beast. His body was a man's; but his head was the head of a bull, and his teeth were the teeth of a lion, and with them he tore his prey. And when he saw Theseus, he roared, and put his head down, and rushed right at him.

But Theseus stepped aside nimbly, and as he passed by, cut him in the knee; and ere he could turn in the narrow path, he followed him, and stabbed him again and again from behind, till the monster fled bellowing wildly; for he never before had felt a wound. And Theseus followed him at full speed, holding the clue of thread in his left hand.

Then on, through cavern after cavern, under dark ribs of sounding stone, and up rough glens and torrent-beds, among the sunless roots of Ida, and to the edge

of the eternal snow, went they, the hunter and the hunted, while the hills bellowed to the monster's bellow.

And at last Theseus came up with him, where he lay panting on a slab among the snows, and caught him by the horns, and forced his head back, and drove the keen sword through his throat.

Then he turned, and went back limping and weary, feeling his way down by the clue of thread, till he came to the mouth of that doleful place; and saw waiting for him, whom but Ariadne!

And he whispered, "It is done!" and showed her the sword; and she laid her finger on her lips and led him to the prison, and opened the doors, and set all the prisoners free, while the guards lay sleeping heavily; for she had silenced them with wine.

Then they fled to their ship together, and leapt on board, and hoisted up the sail; and the night lay dark around them, so that they passed through Minos's ships, and escaped all safe to Naxos; and there Ariadne became Theseus's wife.

But that fair Ariadne never came to Athens with her husband. Some say that Theseus left her sleeping on Naxos among the Cyclades; and that Dionysus the wine-king found her, and took her up into the sky. And some say that Dionysus drove away Theseus, and took Ariadne from him by force; but however that may be, in his haste or in his grief, Theseus forgot to put up the white sail. Now Aegeus his father sat and watched on Sunium, day after day, and strained his old eyes across the sea to see the ship from afar. And when he saw the black sail, and not the white one, he gave up Theseus for dead, and in his grief he fell into the sea, and died; so it is called the Aegean to this day.

And now Theseus was king of Athens, and he guarded it and ruled it well.

Swing High, Swing Low

Margaret Greaves

Melanie was growing tired. It was fun to stay for the first time in the great empty house where her uncle was caretaker, and to be shown all over it. But there seemed no end to the grand rooms.

"And this," said Uncle Arthur, "was Hester's room."

Melanie stared as he opened yet another door. This one was different. It was a child's play-room. There was a rocking-horse in one corner, a small desk under the window.

A toy-cupboard stood open, showing a jumble of things inside. They all looked rather old-fashioned. On the floor lay a big green ball, covered with small pictures of children in frilly dresses or knickerbocker suits, playing various games. The shiny surface was cracked and worn in places.

"It looks as if someone's just left it," said Melanie.

"It's a sad story," said Aunt Clara. "Hester lived here more than a hundred years ago. One day she ran out to play in the garden and never came back. They searched and searched, but never found a sign of her or any clue about what could have happened."

"Her parents left her room waiting for her, just as it was," added Uncle Arthur, "and it became a sort of tradition in the family. No one else has ever disturbed it."

"Ugh! Creepy!" said Melanie.

After lunch she was free to explore the gardens. She went very quietly down the terrace steps and across the wide lawn. It was a hot, still, sunlit day, and it seemed wrong to break the silence. Everything was too big and imposing – the great house looming behind her, the stone urns, the flowerbeds where the late summer flowers hung their heavy heads in the drowsy air. The lawn ended in a tall clipped hedge, with an archway in the middle.

Melanie drew a sigh of relief as she slipped through it. This place was much more friendly. A path led into a small paved garden with a pool at its centre. More clipped hedges surrounded it, and through another archway she came into a half-wild area set with trees and shrubs. A swing hung temptingly from a branch of the biggest tree.

Melanie perched herself on the seat, gripped the ropes, and began to swing. Higher and faster she went till it felt like flying, and her own movement made a little breeze in the windless afternoon. At last she tired, rocked gently to a standstill, and went back to look at the pool. For a long time she lay on her stomach on the warm grey stone, watching the darting goldfish and the dragonflies skimming the water-lilies.

There was a rustle beyond the hedge, a whisper, the ghost of a laugh. Melanie sat up quickly. There was someone in the wild garden. She got up quietly, tiptoed to the archway, and peeped through. There was no one there. She ran and hunted between the trees, but still she was alone. She had just turned to leave when she noticed the swing. It was rocking gently to and fro, as if someone had only just left it . . .

"Aunt Clara," asked Melanie at tea-time, "are any other children allowed in the gardens?"

"My gracious, no," said Aunt Clara. "Why do you ask?"

"Oh, I don't know," said Melanie carelessly. "I just thought I heard someone. But I must have imagined it."

As soon as she could next day, she went back to the wild garden. Of course there was no one there but herself and a whistling blackbird. Melanie climbed into the swing and sang to herself as she rushed through the air and the ground rose and fell beneath her.

After a while she went back to the pool. She sat, leaning on one hand, to look down into it. It lay smooth and bright as a mirror, and she could see her own face reflected. She watched it idly for a moment, then glanced away at the flash of a dragonfly. When she looked back there was another face beside hers in the water. A boy's face, thin and laughing. And now another, on the other side of her, as if someone was peering over her shoulder. Melanie gasped with shock, and a startled fish jumped and shattered the still water.

She leapt to her feet.

"Who are you? Who are you?"

No one answered. There was no one there.

"Don't be silly," Melanie said severely to herself. "Of course it was only leaf shadows."

She didn't admit that there were no trees close to the pool which could have cast any shadow. She peeped through the archway at the swing. It was swaying quite gently. Someone laughed. Or was it only that whistling blackbird?

For the next three days Melanie avoided the garden. There were plenty of other things to do. But on the last evening of her stay she told herself not to be ridiculous. She crossed the lawn as the light was already fading into the green-scented dusk of high summer. The pool waited, quietly, harmlessly. She passed by it into the garden beyond.

She heard the creak of the rope as the swing rocked. She felt, even before she saw, that there were people there. A long-legged girl came smiling from behind a tree. In the failing light her hair seemed green as the dusk. Another leaned down from a branch with a little crowing laugh of welcome. The thin-faced boy was suddenly at her side. Out of the corner of her eye she saw others moving.

"We've been waiting for you," said the thin-faced boy.

"For ever so long," said one of the girls. "It's been ages since we had someone like you to play with."

"Catch-as-catch-can," called another voice. "Come on."

A wave of happiness swept over Melanie. Whoever these people were she felt they were friends. She laughed aloud and began to run, chasing and chased, between the trees, round to the pool, back to the trees again. At last, gasping for breath, she grabbed at the swing.

"Stop! Stop a minute!" she begged. "I can't run any more."

Her companions stopped. It was difficult to see them clearly. Some of them seemed almost like part of the trees.

"Who are you?" asked Melanie. "Where do you come from?"

"We belong here, of course," said one of them. "We were here before the house was built."

"Don't you know it's called Oakhill?" asked another. "You know the rhyme.

> Fairy folk
> Do live in oak."

"*Fairies?*" whispered Melanie.

"Maybe. Maybe not. But this land is ours. Stay with us, Melanie."

"What do you mean?"

"You like us, don't you? Stay with us. Play with us. Stay! Stay!"

Melanie felt a confused sense of happiness and longing. The air seemed heavy with all the scents of summer, it trembled with bird calls. She held out her hands and other hands closed over them.

"She's ours! Ours!" exulted the thin-faced boy. "Let's have another game. Here!"

Something bounced and rolled to her feet. She picked it up. It was a ball. There was just enough light left to show the little pictures that covered it. It was smaller, but just like the one she had seen five days ago – a small ball made to match the big one in the deserted play-room. Fear froze her into stillness.

"It's *Hester's* ball!" she whispered. "You! It was *you* who stole her away!"

"She was happy with us. So happy!" said one of the girls. "You will be happy too, Melanie. Come!"

86

Once again her hands touched Melanie's. They were no longer warm, but cold and clinging as water-weeds. With a sharp cry Melanie turned and fled – through the arch, across the paved garden, over the lawn. For a few moments she felt herself pursued by shrill mocking calls and clutching hands that melted into air, but they followed no further than the pool.

At the foot of the terrace she stopped and looked back, a stitch in her side. Were those really dancing figures in the distance – or tree shadows moving in the light wind that comes just before dark? Was it chill laughter that she heard – or only the first owl-calls?

She hurried in and up to the sitting-room, glad to see that the lights were already switched on.

"Why, Melanie!" exclaimed Aunt Clara. "You look as if you'd seen a ghost."

"No, not a ghost," said Melanie.

What was the use of trying to explain? It was more than a hundred years since Hester had played on the swing in the wild garden. There was no one to grieve for her now.

Patrick Comes to School

Margaret Mahy

"Graham," said the teacher, "will you look after Patrick at play time? Remember he is new to the school and has no friends here yet."

There were lots of things Graham would rather have done, but he had to smile and say, "Yes, Mr Porter."

Behind him Harry Biggs gave his funny, grunting laugh and whispered, "Nursey-nursey Graham." Mr Porter was watching, so Graham could not say anything back.

Patrick was a little shrimp of a boy with red hair – not just carroty or ginger – a sort of fiery red. Freckles were all over his face, crowded like people on a five o'clock bus, all jostling and pushing to get the best places. In fact, Graham thought, Patrick probably had more freckles than face. As well as red hair and freckles, Patrick had a tilted nose and eyes so blue and bright that he looked all the time as if he'd just been given a specially good Christmas present. He seemed cheerful, which was something, but he was a skinny, short little fellow, not likely to be much good at sport, or at looking after himself in a fight.

"Just my luck to get stuck with a new boy!" thought Graham.

At play time he took Patrick round and showed him the football field and the shelter shed. Graham's friend, Len, came along too. Len and Graham were very polite to Patrick, and he was very polite back, but it wasn't much fun really. Every now and then Len and Graham would look at each other over Patrick's head. It was easy to do, because he was so small. "Gosh, what a nuisance!" the looks said, meaning Patrick.

Just before the bell went, Harry Biggs came up with three other boys. Harry Biggs *was* big, and the three other boys were even bigger, and came from another class.

"Hello, here's the new boy out with his nurse," said Harry. "What's your name, new boy?"

Graham felt he ought to do something to protect little Patrick, but Patrick spoke out quite boldly and said, "Patrick Fingall O'Donnell." So that was all right.

Harry Biggs frowned at the name. "Now don't be too smart!" he said. "We tear cheeky little kids apart in this school, don't we?" He nudged the other boys, who grinned and shuffled. "Where do you live, O'Donnell?"

Then Patrick said a funny thing. "I live in a house among the trees, and we've got a golden bird sitting on our gate."

He didn't sound as if he was joking. He spoke carefully as if he was asking Harry Biggs a difficult riddle. He sounded as if, in a minute, he might be laughing at Harry Biggs. Harry Biggs must have thought so too, because he frowned even harder and said, "Remember what I told you, and don't be too clever. Now listen . . . what does your father do?"

"Cut it out, Harry," said Graham quickly. "Pick on someone your own size."

"I'm not hurting him, Nursey!" exclaimed Harry. "Go on, Ginger, what does he do for a crust?"

Patrick answered quickly, almost as if he was reciting a poem.

"My father wears clothes with gold all over them," said Patrick. "In the morning he says to the men 'I'll have a look at my elephants this morning,' and he goes and looks at his elephants. When he says the word, the elephants kneel down. He can ride the elephants all day if he wants to, but mostly he is too busy with the lions or his monkeys or his bears."

Harry Biggs stared at Patrick with his eyes popping out of his head.

"Who do you think you're kidding?" he

said at last. "Are you making out your dad's a king or something? Nobody wears clothes with gold on them."

"My father does!" said Patrick. "Wears them every day!" He thought for a moment. "All these lions and tigers lick his hands," he added.

"Does he work in a circus?" asked one of the other boys.

"No!" said Patrick. "We'd live in a caravan then, not a house with a golden bird at the gate." Once again Graham felt that Patrick was turning his answers into riddles.

Before anyone could say any more, the bell rang for them to go back into school.

"Gee, you'll hear all about that!" Len said to Patrick. "Why did you tell him all that stuff?"

"It's true," Patrick said. "He asked me, and it's true."

"He'll think you were taking the mickey," Graham said. "Anyway, it couldn't be true."

"It *is* true," said Patrick, "and it isn't taking the mickey to say what's true, is it?"

"Well, I don't know," Graham muttered

to Len. "It doesn't sound very true to me."

Of course Harry Biggs and the other boys spread the story round the school.

Children came up to Patrick and said, "Hey, does your father wear pure gold?"

"Not all gold," said Patrick. "Just quite a lot."

Then the children would laugh and pretend to faint with laughing.

"Hey, Ginger!" called Harry Biggs. "How's all the elephants?"

"All right, thank you," Patrick would reply politely. Once he added, "We've got a monkey too, at present, and he looks just like you." But he only said it once, because Harry Biggs pulled his hair and twisted his ears. Patrick's ears were nearly as red as his hair.

"Serves you right for showing off," said Graham.

"Well, I might have been showing off a bit," Patrick admitted. "It's hard not to sometimes."

Yet, although they teased him, slowly

children came to like Patrick. Graham liked him a lot. He was so good-tempered and full of jokes. Even when someone was laughing at him, he laughed too. The only thing that worried Graham was the feeling that Patrick was laughing at some secret joke, or at any rate at some quite different thing.

"Don't you get sick of being teased?" he asked.

"Well, I'm a bit sick of it now," Patrick said, "but mostly I don't mind. Anyhow, what I said was true, and that's all there is to say."

"I'd hate to be teased so much," Graham said. But he could see Patrick was like a rubber ball – the harder you knocked him down, the faster and higher he bounced back.

The wonderful day came when the class was taken to the Zoo. Even Harry Biggs, who usually made fun of school outings, looked forward to this one.

Off they went in the school bus, and Mr Porter took them round.

". . . like the Pied Piper of Hamelin,"

said Patrick, "with all the rats following him."

"Who are you calling a rat, Ginger?" said Harry Biggs sourly.

Everywhere at the Zoo was the smell of animals, birds and straw. They had a map which showed them the quickest way to go round the Zoo, and the first lot of cages they went past held birds. There were all sizes and colours of birds from vultures to canaries. One cage held several bright parrots. The parrots watched the children pass with round, wise eyes. Then suddenly the biggest of the lot flew from his perch and clung to the wire peering out at them.

"Patrick! Hallo, Patrick dear!" it said. "Hallo! Hallo! Hallo, Patrick! Hallo, dear!"

Mr Porter looked at Patrick.

"Oh yes," he said. "I forgot about you, Patrick. It's a bit of a busman's holiday for you, isn't it?"

As they walked away the parrot went on screaming after them, "Hallo, Patrick! Patrick! Hallo, dear!" in its funny, parrot voice.

On they went past the lions and tigers. Len and Graham stole sideways glances at Patrick, and so did Harry Biggs and several other children. Patrick looked as wide-eyed and interested as anyone else. He did not seem to see the glances at all.

They went past the bear pits, and then up a hill where there was nothing but trees. Among the trees, beside a stone fence, was a little house. On one of the gate posts was a brass peacock, polished until it shone, and below that was a little notice saying "Head Keeper's Cottage".

Now, for the first time, Patrick suddenly turned and grinned at Graham.

"*That*'s where I live," he whispered.

They were all looking into the bear pits ten minutes later when a man came hurrying to meet them. He was wearing a lot of gold braid all over his blue uniform. There was gold braid round his cap and his brass buttons shone like little suns. His eyes were blue and bright and his face was covered with freckles – more freckle than face you might have said. He stopped to speak to Mr Porter and took off his cap.

His hair was as red as fire.

"Is *that* your father?" Graham asked.

"Yes," said Patrick. "See, I told you he wore a lot of gold."

"Huh!" said Harry Biggs. "Well, why didn't you say when I asked you ... why didn't you say he was a keeper at the Zoo?"

"Head Keeper!" said Graham, feeling suddenly very proud of Patrick.

"Ordinary keepers don't have gold," Patrick pointed out.

"Why didn't you say?" Harry repeated. "Trying to be clever, eh?"

"I don't like things to sound too ordinary," said Patrick, sounding rather self-satisfied. "I like them to be noble and sort of mysterious."

"Well, you're mad," said Harry, but no one was taking any notice of him. Mr Porter and Mr O'Donnell, Head Keeper, came back to them.

"This is Mr O'Donnell," said Mr Porter.

"He has offered to let us have a look at the young lion cubs. They aren't on view to the public yet, so we are very lucky. And don't worry – the mother lion won't be there, so none of you will get eaten."

As they went on their way a foolish little girl said to Patrick, "Have you got any other relatives who do interesting things, Patrick?"

"Shut up!" said Graham, but it was too late.

"My uncle," said Patrick, without any hesitation.

"He's my great-uncle really, though. He eats razor blades for a living, razor blades and burning matches."

"No one can eat razor blades!" shouted Harry Biggs.

"Well, my great-uncle does," said Patrick and this time everyone believed him.

PS. Patrick's great-uncle was a magician.

The Rajah's Ears

Michael Rosen

Once, long ago in India when there were kings called rajahs and people lived in fear of them, there was a rajah who had very big ears. They were so big he wore a special hat to hide them. All day and every day he wore his hat so that no one would know about his ears. Of course, one or two people did know about them, but they didn't say a word to anyone else about it. They could imagine what terrible things would happen to them if the rajah ever found out that they had been gossiping about him.

The rajah was going to get married and so he wanted to have his hair cut.

He ordered a barber to come to the palace, and when he arrived he sent all his servants and courtiers outside.

Then he said to the barber,

"Now listen here, young man, in a moment I am going to take my hat off. Then you will see that I have ears that are not small. No one in the whole country knows about my ears. If ever I hear that you have been talking about my ears, gossiping or telling tales, then I shall cut your head off. If I ever hear that anyone knows about my ears, I will know that you told them, and I will do as I say, I will cut your head off. Do you understand?"

"Yes, your majesty," said the barber.

The rajah took his hat off and the barber cut his hair. All the time he was cutting away with his scissors, he was trying not to look at the rajah's ears. But they were right in front of him all the time, just where he was looking.

So he said over and over again to himself,

"I must not tell anyone about the rajah's ears, I must not tell anyone about the rajah's ears."

When he had finished, the rajah put his hat on and sent the barber off saying, "Remember what I said, young man."

"Yes, your majesty, not a word to anyone."

And that's the way it was, for the rest of the day; he didn't breathe a word about it to anyone at all. But all the time, the barber was thinking about it. At work, the next day, when he was cutting other people's hair, and chatting with a customer, he was thinking about it. The customer says, "I don't suppose much happens to you here, does it? Day in, day out, cutting people's hair?"

Straightaway, the thought of the rajah's big ears leapt into his mind. "Well, sir," he says, "the other day I was cutting the rajah's hair and you won't believe it but you know he's got enormous—"

And he stopped himself. What am I

saying? he thought, I'll get my head cut off.

"What's he got?" said the customer.

"Enormous jewels on his rings," said the barber.

Phew, that was a close one, he said to himself.

At home that night, his wife was changing her earrings and he found himself saying, "Those earrings look very nice on you, my dear."

"Thank you," says his wife, "you don't think they're too small?"

"They don't look too small on you dear, but I tell you who they *would* look funny on – that's the rajah because he's got really big ear—"

What am I saying? he said to himself. I'll get my head cut off.

"What's he got?" said the wife.

"He's got really big earrings. Small ones would look funny on him."

Phew, that was another close one, he thought.

Outside in the yard, his children were

playing and he went out to call them in for bedtime.

Two of them were pulling faces at each other, sticking their tongues out and pulling their ears.

"Don't do that," says the barber, "you look like the rajah."

"Why do we look like the rajah?" says one.

"Because he's got big—"

What am I saying? the barber thought, I'll get my head cut off.

"He's got big children," said the barber, "and they look like the rajah. You look like his children ... so you look like the rajah."

Phew, that was another close one.

And so it went on all the next day. He was dying to tell someone. In the end he had a plan. The next morning, instead of going straight to work, he went off to the woods.

I know what I'll do, he thought, I'll tell a tree. I'll tell a tree that the rajah's got big ears and that'll be that. It won't bother me any more. I'll have told someone who can't tell anyone else. The rajah will never find out, and I'll feel a lot better.

So the barber crept up to a great big tree in the woods. He looked behind him and to either side. He looked behind the tree and all around it and then he stood up in front of it and said,

"The rajah's got big ears."

Oooh, that felt so much better. It felt like a great load had been taken off his back and off he went to work happier than he had been for days.

Later that day, a woodcutter came to the woods and chopped down the very same tree that the barber had talked to. The woodcutter sold the wood from the tree to a musical instrument maker and the instrument maker made some drums called tabla and a stringed instrument called a sitar.

The instrument maker sold the tabla and sitar to a band that was one of the best in the country. In fact, so good was this band, that they were asked to play at the rajah's wedding.

Everyone was there, all the rajah's relations, all his servants, all his servants' servants, even the rajah's barber.

What a day it was. There was a wonderful ceremony, followed by a great feast and then came the dance.

The musicians made ready, there was a hush and then the music began.

But of all surprising and awful things to happen, the sound coming out of the musical instruments wasn't a wedding dance but a song, and the words of the song were:

> *"The rajah's got big ears,*
> *oh yes the rajah's got big ears,*
> *do you know what*
> *I know what*
> *The rajah's got big ears."*

"Stop, stop, stop," shouted the rajah.

"I heard that," he roared, "I heard every word of that."

The hundreds of wedding guests stood in silence.

The thought of his barber sprang into the rajah's mind. Only the barber knew about his ears, only the barber could have told anyone.

"BARBER!" bellowed the rajah, "barber, where are you?"

The barber stepped forward.

"Yes, your majesty?"

"I heard that song. You heard that song. You have disobeyed me. I told you not to tell a single person and now everyone knows."

"But your majesty, I didn't tell a single person."

"Oh yes you did, and tonight you lose your head."

"But, your majesty, I didn't tell a single person. I told a tree. That's not a person, is it?"

The rajah stopped. A smile crept on to his face.

He muttered to himself.

"'I didn't tell a person. I told a tree.' The man's right, he didn't tell a single person. Oh, what am I making a fuss about? It's only ears. So what if I have got big ears? Some people have got big feet, some people have got little noses. We're all different and we always will be."

At that, he pulled off his hat and said,

"Friends and relations, the rajah's got big ears. Let the band play."

The band played and everyone sang.

> *"The rajah's got big ears,*
> *oh yes the rajah's got big ears*
> *do you know what*
> *I know what*
> *The rajah's got big ears."*

Strange Animal

Alexander McCall Smith

There were many people to tell that boy
what to do. There was his mother and his
father, his grandfather, and his older brother.
And there was also an aunt, who was always
saying "Do this. Do that." Every day this
aunt would shout at him, and make a great
noise that would frighten the birds.

The boy did not like his aunt. Sometimes
he thought that he might go to some man to
buy some medicine to put into her food to
make her quiet, but of course he never did

this. In spite of all his aunt's shouting and ordering about, the boy always obeyed her, as his father said he must.

"She has nothing to do but shout at you," the boy's father explained. "It keeps her happy."

"When I'm a big man I'll come and shout in her ear," the boy said. It was good to think about that.

There was a place that the aunt knew where a lot of fruit grew. It was a place which was quite far away, and the boy did not like going there. Near this place there were caves, and the boy had heard that a strange animal lived in these caves. One of his friends had seen this strange animal and had warned people about going near that place.

But the aunt insisted on sending the boy to pick fruit there, and so he went, his heart a cold stone of fear inside him. He found the trees and began to pick the fruit, but a little later he heard the sound of something in the bush beside him. He stopped his task and stood near the tree in case the strange animal should be coming.

Out of the bush came the strange animal. It was just as his friend had described it and the boy was very frightened. Quickly he took out the drum which he had brought with him and began to beat it. The strange animal stopped, looked at the boy in surprise, and began to dance.

All day the boy played the drum, keeping the strange animal dancing. As long as he played the drum, he knew that there was nothing that the strange animal could do to harm him. At last, when night came, the strange animal stopped dancing and disappeared back into the bush. The boy knew that it had gone back to its cave and so he was able to walk home safely. When he reached home, though, his aunt had prepared her shouting.

"Where is all the fruit?" she shouted. Thinking that he had eaten it, she then began to beat him until the boy was able to run away from her and hide in his own hut.

The boy told his father the next day of the real reason why he had been unable to bring back fruit from the tree. He explained that there had been a strange animal there and that he had had to play his drum to keep the animal dancing. The father listened and told the story to the aunt, who scoffed at the boy.

"There are no strange animals at that place," she said. "You must be making all this up."

But the father believed the boy and said that the next day they would all go to the fruit place with him. The aunt thought that this was a waste of time, but she was not going to miss any chance of shouting, and so she came too.

When all the family reached the tree there was no strange animal. The aunt began to pick fruit from the tree and stuff it into her mouth. Calling to the boy to give her his drum, she hung it on the branch of a tree in a place where he would not be able to get at it easily.

"You must pick fruit," she shouted to

the boy. "You must not play a drum in idleness."

The boy obeyed his aunt, but all the time he was listening for any sounds to come from the bush. He knew that sooner or later the strange animal would appear and that they would then all be in danger.

When the strange animal did come, it went straight to the boy's father and mother and quickly ate them up. Then the aunt tried to run away, but the strange animal ran after her and ate her too. While this was happening, the boy had time to reach up for his drum from the branch of the fruit tree. Quickly he began to play this drum, which made the strange animal stop looking for people to eat and begin to dance.

As the boy played his drum faster and faster, the strange animal danced more and more quickly. Eventually the boy played so fast that the animal had to spit out the father and the mother. The boy was very pleased with this and began to play more slowly. At this, the strange animal's dancing became slower.

"You must play your drum fast again," the boy's father said. "Then the strange animal will have to spit out your aunt."

"Do I have to?" the boy asked, disappointed that he would not be allowed to leave the aunt in the stomach of the strange animal.

"Yes," the boy's father said sternly. "You must."

Reluctantly, the boy again began to play the drum and the strange animal began to dance more quickly. After a few minutes it was dancing so quickly that it had to spit out the aunt. Then darkness came and the strange animal went back to its cave.

The aunt was very quiet during the journey back home. The next day she was quiet as well, and she never shouted at the boy again. Being swallowed by a strange animal had taught the aunt not to waste her time shouting; now, all that she wanted to do was to sit quietly in the sun.

The boy was very happy.

Vardiello

Retold by Geoffrey Summerfield

There was once a very sensible woman who lived with her only son. His name was Vardiello, and he was a real fool.

One day, the mother had to run an errand, so she said to her silly lad: "Now, listen. I've got to go out for an hour or two. The old hen in the shed is sitting on a dozen eggs, and they should be hatching out soon. So you must make sure she stays on the eggs and keeps them warm. If she wanders off to go scratching about in the yard, just look sharp and see that she gets back to the nest, double quick. Or we shall have no chickens. You understand?"

"Don't you worry about a thing. I'll take care of everything."

"And one more thing. That new pot in the cupboard. If you so much as nibble what's in that pot, you'll be dead before you can say Jack Robinson. So leave well alone."

"Thanks for the warning. I'll go nowhere near it."

Now, as soon as his mother had gone, Vardiello went into the garden, and he dug holes all over, and covered them with twigs and clods, to try to catch the lads that used to come scrumping in the apple trees. He worked hard for an hour or more, and he was just rubbing his aching back when he saw the old hen come waddling into the garden for a good scratch around.

"Back you go! Shoo! Shoo! Hish! Hish! Back to your eggs! Go on!"

But the hen just ignored him. So he stamped his feet. Then he threw his cap at her. But it made no difference. The old hen just went on with her scratching. So Vardiello got into a real panic, and he picked up a big stick and threw it at her!

Bonk! It hit the poor old hen right on the head, and there she lay, in the dust, dead as a doornail.

"Oh, the eggs! The chickens!" Vardiello cried. And he rushed into the shed. He put his hand on the eggs and they were almost stone-cold. So he sat on them, to warm them up again, and his trousers were plastered with smashed eggs. What a mess! He tried to scrape it all off, but his hands were just smeared with goo, so he wriggled out of his trousers and washed them in the kitchen sink. He didn't have time to dry them, and they were his only pair, so he put them on again while they were still sopping wet, and his legs felt clammy from top to bottom.

By this time, he was so hungry that his stomach was rumbling like thunder. So he went out and found the poor old hen. He plucked her and cleaned her, lit a fire in the grate, and cooked her.

When the old hen was well cooked, he

put her just outside the kitchen door to cool off. Then he decided to do himself proud, and spread a clean cloth on the table. Then he went down to the cellar with a large jug to get some wine to drink with his meal: in those days, people didn't drink tea, but used to keep a great barrel of wine in the cellar, to drink with their meals.

So he put his jug under the tap of the barrel, and turned the tap on. He was watching all the bubbles sparkling in the jug, when he heard a terrible clattering and banging upstairs. So he rushed out of the cellar, and there were two great tom-cats fighting over his chicken!

He chased those cats all over the yard, and they dashed into the house to hide. So he chased them all over the house, upstairs and downstairs, until the cats dropped the old hen under the bed. By the time he'd picked it up and cleaned it, he suddenly remembered the wine-tap: it was still running!

So he dashed down to the cellar, and the barrel was empty. The wine was all over the floor, a great flood. Now he had to work out

a plan to prevent his mother from finding out. He took a sack of flour, and scattered it all over the cellar floor, to soak up all the wine.

Then he sat down, and thought. "No fat hen! No eggs! No chickens! No wine! No flour! No hope!"

He didn't dare face his mother when she came back, so he decided to do away with himself. He remembered what she had said about the new pot in the cupboard. She'd said he would die if he even nibbled whatever was in that pot. So he rushed up out of the cellar, slipping and sliding on the flour paste on the floor, and rushed to the cupboard. He snatched the pot off the shelf and gulped down everything, glug, glug, munch, munch, until the pot was empty.

Then he went and hid in the oven, and waited to die.

When his mother got back, she knocked and knocked. She had always told him to lock the door when she went out, so she waited for him to come and open it. She knocked and knocked, then she knocked again until her knuckles were sore. Then she lost her patience and kicked the door open.

"Vardiello! Vardiello! Where are you? What are you up to? Are you deaf? Come out, come out, wherever you are! Do you hear?"

And a thin squeaky voice came out of the oven: "I'm in here. In the oven. But you'll never see me again. I shall be dead in a minute!"

"Don't talk daft!"

"But I shall. I've eaten the poison in the pot. And I'm dying."

Then his mother sat down and laughed until she cried. The tears poured down her face, and her handkerchief was soaking wet.

"Tell me all about it," she said, when she could speak. "You silly billy! Tell me what happened."

So he told her all about the old hen, the eggs, the cats, the wine, the flour, and the poison in the pot.

"Oh, the pot!" his mother said. "It was

full of pickled walnuts. I was saving them for a rainy day. I just didn't want you to eat them. So I warned you to leave well alone! But they weren't poison. You'll just have a stomach ache. Now come out of that oven and stretch your legs."

So Vardiello clambered out of the oven. And he felt very foolish. Then his mother gave him a glass of milk.

"Now, what are we going to do for food?" she asked him. "No eggs. No chickens. No hen. No flour. No wine. Dear me, I shall have to sell that cloth I've been weaving."

So she went up to her bedroom and came down with her arms full of a great roll of fine cloth.

"Take this into the market and sell it," she told Vardiello. "But be careful. People who talk a lot, and use big words, are probably trying to cheat you. So be on your guard."

"Don't you worry about a thing," Vardiello told his mother, and carried the cloth off to market. "Cloth! Fine cloth!" he shouted. But whenever anybody said "I'd like to buy some of your cloth," he remembered what his mother had said. They talk too much, he thought, so he didn't sell even a square inch, for fear of being cheated. "Cloth! Cloth!" he shouted, over and over again, for hours on end, until he was worn out. Then he wandered off, out of the market-place, until he came to a statue. His feet were sore by this time, that he sat on the ground to rest, and leaned against the statue.

"A customer!" he thought, looking at the statue. "He could do with some cloth to make some new clothes."

"Would you like to buy some cloth?" he asked the statue. No reply.

"It's very good. Don't you like the look of it?" No reply.

"This is the man for me," Vardiello whispered.

"It will suit you, sir," he said to the statue. "I'll leave it with you. Then you can have a good look at it. You can pay me tomorrow. I'll come back then."

Then he rushed home to tell his mother all about his success.

"Oh, you idiot! You can't be trusted

to do anything! What am I going to do with you?"

"But, but, Mother, wait till tomorrow. You'll see. I'll get the money for your cloth. Just wait and see."

The next day, Vardiello rushed off to collect his money from the statue. He had left the cloth by the feet of the statue and, of course, the first person to pass that way had walked off with it.

"I've come for my money. The money for the cloth I left with you yesterday."

The statue said nothing.

"My money!" Vardiello shouted. "Money for the cloth."

The statue said not a word.

"My money!" Vardiello shouted. He was almost weeping with anger by this time, and he rushed to pick up a brick and hurled it at the statue.

And lo and behold, the statue smashed to smithereens! And inside the broken statue, Vardiello found a pot full of gold coins.

Vardiello snatched it up, and laughed out loud. Then he ran all the way home.

"Mother! Mother! Payment! Money for the cloth!"

When his mother saw the pot full of gold coins she was amazed. Then she thought, "Vardiello is going to tell everybody about this gold. I must do something, quick!"

"Thank you, son. Put it all in the cupboard. Then go to the front door and wait for the milkman. I don't want to miss him."

So Vardiello went and sat just outside the front door. And his mother went upstairs, opened the bedroom window, and dropped a shower of nuts and raisins, currants, figs, and dates on the lad. Vardiello couldn't believe his eyes. He caught them in his hands and in his mouth, then he called out to his mother.

"Mother! Mother! It's raining figs, and dates, and nuts, and raisins! Bring a bowl! Quick!"

So his mother slipped downstairs very

quietly on tiptoe and collected her nuts and dates and the currants and raisins in a bowl. And she let Vardiello eat till he was fit to burst, and fell asleep.

A few weeks later, two men were arguing in the street. One of them had found a gold coin in his back garden, and his neighbour was trying to claim it for his own. Vardiello heard them and said, "Ridiculous! Arguing about a single gold coin! I found a whole potful of them!"

So the men dragged him off to the police station, and the chief of police said to Vardiello. "Now, my young man, tell me all about your pot of gold."

"It's very simple, sir. I found it a few weeks ago inside a dumb man who stole a roll of my mother's cloth, on the day it rained figs, and raisins, and currants, and nuts, and . . ."

"A fine tail our cat's got," said the chief of police. "Now, run along, my lad, and don't let your imagination run away with you!"

And Vardiello and his mother lived happily ever after. Whenever they needed food, they took a coin out of the pot in their cupboard, and nobody ever believed a word of Vardiello's story.

The Cat That Walked by Himself

Rudyard Kipling

Hear and attend and listen; for this befell and behappened and became and was, O my Best Beloved, when the tame animals were wild. The Dog was wild, and the Horse was wild, and the Cow was wild, and the Sheep was wild, and the Pig was wild – as wild as wild could be – and they walked in the Wet Wild Woods by their wild lones. But the wildest of all the wild animals was the Cat. He walked by himself, and all places were alike to him.

Of course the Man was wild too. He was dreadfully wild. He didn't even begin to be tame till he met the Woman, and she told him that she did not like living in his Wild ways. She picked out a nice dry Cave, instead of a heap of wet leaves, to lie down in; and she strewed clean sand on the floor; and she lit a nice fire of wood at the back of the Cave; and she hung a dried wild-horse skin, tail-down, across the opening of the Cave; and she said, "Wipe your feet, dear, when you come in, and now we'll keep house."

That night, Best Beloved, they ate wild sheep roasted on the hot stones, and flavoured with wild garlic and wild pepper; and wild duck stuffed with wild rice and wild fenugreek and wild coriander; and marrow-bones of wild oxen; and wild cherries, and wild grenadillas. Then the Man went to sleep in front of the fire very happy; but the Woman sat up, combing her hair. She took the bone of the shoulder of mutton – the big flat blade-bone – and she looked at the wonderful marks on it, and she threw more wood on the fire, and she made a Magic. She made the First Singing Magic in the world.

Out in the Wet Wild Woods all the wild animals gathered together where they could see the light of the fire a long way off, and they wondered what it meant.

Then Wild Horse stamped with his wild foot and said, "O my Friends and O my Enemies, why have the Man and the Woman made that great light in that great Cave, and what harm will it do us?"

Wild Dog lifted up his wild nose and smelled the smell of the roast mutton, and said, "I will go up and see and look, and say; for I think it is good. Cat, come with me."

"Nenni!" said the Cat. "I am the Cat who walks by himself, and all places are alike to me. I will not come."

"Then we can never be friends again," said Wild Dog, and he trotted off to the Cave. But when he had gone a little way the Cat said to himself. "All places are alike to me. Why should I not go too and see and look and come away at my own liking?"

So he slipped after Wild Dog softly, very softly, and hid himself where he could hear everything.

When Wild Dog reached the mouth of the Cave he lifted up the dried horse-skin with his nose and sniffed the beautiful smell of the roast mutton, and the Woman, looking at the blade-bone, heard him, and laughed, and said, "Here comes the first. Wild Thing out of the Wild Woods, what do you want?"

Wild Dog said, "O my Enemy and Wife of my Enemy, what is this that smells so good in the Wild Woods?"

Then the Woman picked up a roasted mutton-bone and threw it to Wild Dog, and said "Wild Thing out of the Wild Woods, taste and try." Wild Dog gnawed the bone, and it was more delicious than anything he had ever tasted, and he said, "O my Enemy and Wife of my Enemy, give me another."

The Woman said, "Wild Thing out of the Wild Woods, help my Man to hunt through the day and guard this Cave at night and

I will give you as many roast bones as you need."

"Ah!" said the Cat, listening. "This is a very wise Woman, but she is not so wise as I am."

Wild Dog crawled into the Cave and laid his head on the Woman's lap, and said, "O my Friend and Wife of my Friend, I will help your Man to hunt through the day, and at night I will guard your Cave."

"Ah!" said the Cat, listening. "This is a very foolish Dog." And he went back through the Wet Wild Woods waving his wild tail, and walking by his wild lone. But he never told anybody.

When the Man waked up he said, "What is Wild Dog doing here?" and the Woman said, "His name is not Wild Dog any more, but the First Friend, because he will be our friend for always and always and always. Take him with you when you go hunting."

Next night the Woman cut great green armfuls of fresh grass from the water-meadows, and dried it before the fire, so that it smelt like new-mown hay, and she

134

sat at the mouth of the Cave and plaited a halter out of horse-hide, and she looked at the shoulder-of-mutton bone – at the big broad blade-bone – and she made a Magic. She made the Second Singing Magic in the world.

Out in the Wild Woods all the wild animals wondered what had happened to Wild Dog, and at last Wild Horse stamped with his foot and said, "I will go and see and say why Wild Dog has not returned. Cat, come with me."

"Nenni!" said the Cat. "I am the Cat who walks by himself, and all places are alike to me. I will not come." But all the same he followed Wild Horse softly, very softly, and hid himself where he could hear everything.

When the Woman heard Wild Horse, tripping and stumbling on his long mane, she laughed and said, "Here comes the second Wild Thing out of the Wild Woods, what do you want?"

Wild Horse said, "O my Enemy and Wife of my Enemy, where is Wild Dog?"

135

The Woman laughed, and picked up the blade-bone and looked at it, and said, "Wild Thing out of the Wild Woods, you did not come here for Wild Dog, but for the sake of this good grass."

And Wild Horse, tripping and stumbling on his long mane, said, "That is true; give it to me to eat."

The Woman said, "Wild Thing out of the Wild Woods, bend your head and wear what I give you, and you shall eat the wonderful grass three times a day."

"Ah!" said the Cat, listening. "This is a clever Woman, but she is not so clever as I am."

Wild Horse bent his wild head, and the Woman slipped the plaited-hide halter over it, and Wild Horse breathed on the Woman's feet and said, "O my Mistress, and Wife of my Master, I will be your servant for the sake of the wonderful grass."

"Ah!" said the Cat, listening, "That is a very foolish Horse." And he went back through the Wet Wild Woods, waving his wild tail and walking by his wild lone. But he never told anybody.

When the Man and the Dog came back from hunting, the Man said, "What is Wild Horse doing here?" And the Woman said, "His name is not Wild Horse any more, but the First Servant, because he will carry us from place to place for always and always and always. Ride on his back when you go hunting."

Next day, holding her wild head high that her wild horns should not catch in the wild trees, Wild Cow came up to the Cave, and the Cat followed, and hid himself just the same as before; and everything happened just the same as before; and the Cat said the same things as before; and when Wild Cow had promised to give her milk to the Woman every day in exchange for the wonderful grass, the Cat went back through the Wet Wild Woods waving his wild tail and walking by his wild lone, just the same as before. But he never told anybody. And when the Man and the Horse and the Dog came home from hunting and asked the same questions same as before, the Woman said, "Her name is not Wild Cow any more, but the Giver of Good Food. She will give us the warm white milk for always and always and always, and I will take care of her while you and the First Friend and the First Servant go hunting."

Next day the Cat waited to see if any other Wild Thing would go up to the Cave, but no one moved in Wet Wild Woods, so the Cat walked there by himself; and he saw the Woman milking the Cow, and he saw the light of the fire in the Cave, and he smelt the smell of the warm white milk.

Cat said, "O my Enemy and Wife of my Enemy, where did Wild Cow go?"

The Woman laughed and said, "Wild Thing out of the Wild Woods, go back to the Woods again, for I have braided up my hair, and I have put away the magic blade-bone, and we have no more need of either friends or servants in our Cave."

Cat said, "I am not a friend, and I am not a servant. I am the Cat who walks by himself, and I wish to come into your cave."

Woman said, "Then why did you not come with First Friend on the first night?"

Cat grew very angry and said, "Has Wild Dog told tales of me?"

Then the woman laughed and said, "You are the Cat who walks by himself, and all places are alike to you. You are neither a friend nor a servant. You have said it yourself. Go away and walk by yourself in all places alike."

Then Cat pretended to be sorry and said, "Must I never come into the Cave? Must I never sit by the warm fire? Must I never drink the warm white milk? You are very wise and very beautiful. You should not be cruel even to a Cat."

Woman said, "I knew I was wise, but I did not know I was beautiful. So I will make a bargain with you. If ever I say one word in your praise, you may come into the Cave."

"And if you say two words in my praise?" said the Cat.

"I never shall," said the Woman, "but if I say two words in your praise, you may sit by the fire in the Cave."

"And if you say three words?" said the Cat.

"I never shall," said the Woman, "but if I say three words in your praise, you may drink the warm white milk three times a day for always and always and always."

Then the Cat arched his back and said, "Now let the Curtain at the mouth of the Cave, and the Fire at the back of the Cave, and the Milk-pots that stand beside the Fire, remember what my Enemy and the Wife of my Enemy has said." And he went away through the Wet Wild Woods waving his wild tail and walking by his wild lone.

That night when the Man and the Horse and the Dog came home from hunting, the Woman did not tell them of the bargain she had made with the Cat, because she was afraid that they might not like it. Cat went far and far away and hid himself in the Wet Wild Woods by his wild lone for a long time till the Woman forgot all about him. Only the Bat – the little upside-down Bat – that hung inside the Cave knew where Cat hid; and every evening Bat would fly to Cat with news of what was happening.

One evening Bat said, "There is a Baby in the Cave. He is new and pink and fat, and the Woman is very fond of him."

"Ah," said the Cat, listening, "but what is the Baby fond of?"

"He is fond of things that are soft and tickle," said the Bat. "He is fond of warm things to hold in his arms when he goes to sleep. He is fond of being played with. He is fond of all those things."

"Ah," said the Cat, listening, "then my time has come."

Next night Cat walked through the Wet Wild Woods and hid very near the Cave till morning, and Man and Dog and Horse went hunting. The Woman was busy cooking that morning, and the Baby cried and interrupted. So she carried him outside the Cave and gave him a handful of pebbles to play with. But still the Baby cried.

Then the Cat put out his paddy paw and patted the Baby on the cheek, and it cooed: and the Cat rubbed against its fat knees and tickled it under its fat chin with his tail. And the Baby laughed; and the Woman heard him and smiled.

Then the Bat – the little upside-down Bat – that hung in the mouth of the Cave said, "O my Hostess and Wife of my Host and Mother of my Host's Son, a Wild Thing from the Wild Woods is most beautifully playing with your Baby."

"A blessing on that Wild Thing whoever he may be," said the Woman, straightening her back, "for I was a busy woman this morning and he has done me a service."

That very minute and second, Best Beloved, the dried horse-skin Curtain that was stretched tail-down at the mouth of the Cave fell down – *woosh*! – because it remembered the bargain she had made with the Cat; and when the Woman went to pick it up – lo and behold! – the Cat was sitting quite comfy inside the Cave.

"O my Enemy and Wife of my Enemy and Mother of my Enemy," said the Cat, "it is I: for you have spoken a word in my praise, and now I can sit within the Cave for always and always and always. But still I am the Cat who walks by himself, and all places are alike to me."

The Woman was very angry, and shut her lips tight and took up her spinning-wheel and began to spin.

But the Baby cried because the Cat had gone away, and the Woman could not hush it, for it struggled and kicked and grew black in the face.

"O my Enemy and Wife of my Enemy and Mother of my Enemy," said the Cat, "take a strand of the thread that you are spinning and tie it to your spinning-whorl and drag it along the floor, and I will show you a Magic that shall make your Baby laugh as loudly as he is now crying."

"I will do so," said the Woman, "because I am at my wits' end; but I will not thank you for it."

She tied the thread to the little clay spindle-whorl and drew it across the floor, and the Cat ran after it and patted it with his paws, and rolled head over heels, and tossed it backward over his shoulder and chased it between his hind legs and pretended to lose it, and pounced down upon it again, till the Baby laughed as loudly as it had been crying, and scrambled after the Cat and frolicked all over the Cave till it grew tired and settled down to sleep with the Cat in its arms.

"Now," said Cat, "I will sing the Baby a song that shall keep him asleep for an hour." And he began to purr, loud and low, low and loud, till the Baby fell fast asleep. The Woman smiled as she looked down upon the two of them, and said, "That was wonderfully done. No question but you are clever, O Cat."

That very minute and second, Best Beloved, the smoke of the Fire at the back of the Cave came down in clouds from the roof – *puff*! – because it remembered the bargain she had made with the Cat; and when it had cleared away – lo and behold! – the Cat was sitting quite comfy close to the fire.

"O my Enemy and Wife of my Enemy and Mother of my Enemy," said the Cat, "it is I: for you have spoken a second word in my praise, and now I can sit by the warm fire at the back of the Cave for always and always and always. But still I am the Cat who walks by himself, and all places are alike to me."

Then the Woman was very very angry, and let down her hair and put some more wood on the fire and brought out the broad blade-bone of the shoulder of mutton and began to make a Magic that should prevent her from saying a third word in praise of the Cat. It was not a Singing Magic, Best Beloved, it was a Still Magic; and by and by the Cave grew so still that a little wee mouse crept out of a corner and ran across the floor.

"O my Enemy and Wife of my Enemy and Mother of my Enemy," said the Cat, "is that little mouse part of your Magic?"

"Ouh! Chee! No indeed!" said the Woman, and she dropped the blade-bone and jumped upon the footstool in front of the fire and braided up her hair very quick for fear that the mouse should run up it.

"Ah," said the Cat, watching, "then the mouse will do me no harm if I eat it?"

"No," said the Woman, braiding up her hair, "eat it quickly and I will ever be grateful to you."

Cat made one jump and caught the little mouse, and the Woman said, "A hundred thanks. Even the First Friend is not quick enough to catch little mice as you have done. You must be very wise."

That very moment and second, O Best Beloved, the Milkpot that stood by the fire cracked in two pieces – *ffft*! – because it remembered the bargain she had made with the Cat; and when the Woman jumped down from the footstool – lo and behold! – the Cat was lapping up the warm white milk that lay in one of the broken pieces.

"O my Enemy and Wife of my Enemy and Mother of my Enemy," said the Cat, "it is I: for you have spoken three words in my praise, and now I can drink the warm white milk three times a day for always and always and always. But *still* I am the Cat who walks by himself, and all places are alike to me."

Then the Woman laughed and set the Cat a bowl of the warm white milk and said, "O Cat, you are as clever as a man, but remember that your bargain was not made with the Man or the Dog, and I do not know what they will do when they come home."

"What is that to me?" said the Cat. "If I have my place in the Cave by the fire and my warm white milk three times a day I do not care what the Man or the Dog can do."

That evening when the Man and the Dog came into the Cave, the Woman told them all the story of the bargain, while the Cat sat by the fire and smiled. Then the Man said, "Yes, but he has not made a bargain with *me* or with all proper Men after me." Then he took off his two leather boots and he took up his little stone axe (that makes three) and he fetched a piece of wood and a hatchet (that is five altogether), and he set them out in a row and he said, "Now we will make *our* bargain. If you do not catch mice when you are in the Cave for always and always and always, I will throw these five things at you whenever I see you, and so shall all proper Men do after me."

"Ah," said the Woman, listening, "this is a very clever Cat, but he is not so clever as my Man."

The Cat counted the five things (and they looked very knobby) and he said, "I will catch mice when I am in the Cave for always and always and always; but *still* I am the Cat who walks by himself, and all places are alike to me."

"Not when I am near," said the Man. "If you had not said that last I would have put all these things away for always and always and always; but now I am going to throw my two boots and my little stone axe (that makes three) at you whenever I meet you. And so shall all proper Men do after me!"

Then the Dog said, "Wait a minute. He has not made a bargain with *me* or with all proper Dogs after me." And he showed his teeth and said, "If you are not kind to the Baby while I am in the Cave for always and always and always, I will hunt you till I catch you, and when I catch you I will bite you. And so shall all proper Dogs do after me."

"Ah," said the Woman, listening, "this is a very clever Cat, but he is not so clever as the Dog."

Cat counted the Dog's teeth (and they looked very pointed) and he said, "I will be kind to the Baby while I am in the Cave, as long as he does not pull my tail too hard, for always and always and always. But *still* I am the Cat that walks by himself, and all places are alike to me."

"Not when I am near," said the Dog. "If you had not said that last I would have shut my mouth for always and always and always; but *now* I am going to hunt you up a tree whenever I meet you. And so shall all proper Dogs do after me."

Then the Man threw his two boots and his little stone axe (that makes three) at the Cat, and the Cat ran out of the Cave and the Dog chased him up a tree; and from that day to this, Best Beloved, three proper Men out of five will always throw things at a Cat whenever they meet him, and all proper Dogs will chase him up a tree. But the Cat keeps his side of the bargain too. He will kill mice, and he will be kind to Babies when he is in the house, just as long as they do not pull his tail too hard. But when he has done that, and between times, and when the moon gets up and night comes he is the Cat that walks by himself, and all places are alike to him. Then he goes out to the Wet Wild Woods or up the Wet Wild Trees or on the Wet Wild Roofs, waving his wild tail and walking by his wild lone.

Big Claus
and Little Claus

Hans Christian Andersen
Translated by Stephen Corrin

Once upon a time there were two men who lived in the same town and had the same name – both were called Claus. But one of them had four horses and the other only one. So to tell one from the other, they called the one who owned four horses Big Claus and the one who owned only one horse Little Claus. And now let's find out how these two got on together, for it really is quite a story.

For six days of the week Little Claus had to do the ploughing for Big Claus and lend him his one horse. In return, Big Claus would help Little Claus with his four horses – but only once a week, on Sundays. And how Little Claus would crack down his whip on all five horses on Sundays, when the horses were his! The sun would shine so bright, the bells in the church would peal out loud and clear and people would walk by in their very best clothes and their hymn books under their arms, on their way to hear the vicar preach his sermon, and they would see Little Claus ploughing away with his five horses. And he would feel so happy that he would bring down his whip with a resounding thwack! and cry: "Gee up there, all my horses."

"Don't SAY that," warned Big Claus. "Only one of them is yours."

But as soon as anyone passed by again on the way to church, Little Claus would forget about this and he would cry out: "Gee up there, all my horses."

"Now stop that at once, if you please,"

warned Big Claus again. "If you say it just once more, I'll crack your horse over the head and kill him dead; and that'll be the end of him."

"I won't say it again, I promise," said Little Claus. But when the people walked by and nodded Good-day he would feel so happy and so grand to have five horses that he would crack his whip and cry out, "Gee up there, all my horses!"

"I'll teach you to gee up your horses," said Big Claus and, taking a mallet, he brought down such a mighty crack on the head of Little Claus's only horse that it fell down dead on the spot.

"Oh dear," wailed Little Claus. "Now I haven't got a horse at all." And he started to cry. But he didn't cry for very long. He stripped the hide off his dead horse and then left the hide to dry in the wind. Then he put it into a bag, threw the bag over his shoulders and set off to sell the horse-hide in the nearest town.

It was a very long way, through a great dark wood, and all of a sudden there was a terrible storm. Little Claus was quite lost and wandered all over the place until at last he found himself outside a large farmhouse. The shutters were up, for it was already night-fall, but he could see a small light shining over the top of them.

"I expect they will put me up for the night," thought Little Claus and he went and knocked at the door.

The farmer's wife opened it. When she heard what he wanted, she said: "You can't come in here. My husband is away and I don't take strangers in." And with that she shut the door in his face.

Little Claus looked around. There was a haystack close by and between that and the farmhouse there was a shed with a flat thatched roof.

"I can sleep up there," thought Little Claus, looking up at the roof. "It should make a fine bed. I don't imagine that stork will fly down and peck my legs" (for, standing on the roof, was a real stork which had built its nest there).

So up he climbed on to the shed and

lay down and wriggled about till he was nice and comfortable. The shutters on the farmhouse windows did not quite fit at the top, so he was able to look over them, right inside, and see what was going on.

He could see a big table spread with roast meat and red wine and some very tasty-looking fish. The farmer's wife and the village schoolmaster were sitting there and she was filling up his glass and he was helping himself to the fish, to which he seemed to be very partial.

"Wouldn't I just like to have some of that!" thought Little Claus, sticking his head as close to the window as he could. "Goodness me, what a splendid cake! What a feast they're having!"

Just then he heard the sound of horses' hooves along the high road. They were coming towards the house; it was the woman's husband coming home. He was a most worthy man but he had one rather strange weakness – he couldn't stand the sight of village schoolmasters. The mere mention of one would send him mad with rage, which was why the schoolmaster was visiting the farmer's wife when her husband was away and why she was now offering him her tastiest dishes. So now, when they heard her husband coming, they both got very frightened and the woman told the schoolmaster to hide in a large empty chest in the corner. Which he did at once, and the woman quickly put away all the delicious food and wine in her oven, for if her husband had seen them he would certainly have asked what it all meant.

"Oh, what a shame," sighed Little Claus from his thatched bed, when he saw all the appetising food disappear into the oven.

"Who is that up there?" called the farmer, looking up at Little Claus. "Why are you lying there? Come indoors with me."

Little Claus then told him about the storm and how he had lost his way and asked the good farmer if he could put him up for the night.

"Most certainly," said the farmer, "but first let's have a bite of supper."

The farmer's wife had now become all

friendly and welcomed Little Claus when she saw him at the door with her husband. She spread the cloth on the long table and served them a large bowl of porridge. The farmer ate heartily enough but Little Claus could not take his mind off the delicious roast meat and fish and the wine and the cake which he knew were in the oven. Under the table at his feet was the bag with the horse-hide. He trod on the bag and the dry hide gave out a loud squeak.

"Hush!" said Little Claus pretending to listen to something, and he trod on it again, making it squeak even louder.

"Hello," said the farmer, "what's that you've got under there?"

"Oh, that's my wizard. I keep him in my bag," replied Little Claus. "He says we are not to eat the porridge for he's conjured the whole oven full of roast meat, fish, cake and red wine."

"What! What!" exclaimed the farmer, and stretching over to the oven, he opened it and saw all the delicious food his wife had hidden away there but which he believed the wizard had conjured up for him.

His wife, not daring to say a word, placed all the food on the table at once and they helped themselves freely. When they had eaten and drunk to their hearts' content, the farmer became quite jolly and asked: "What else can your wizard do? Can he call up the Devil, I wonder? I'd like to see him do that."

"Oh yes," said Little Claus, "my wizard will do anything I ask – won't you?" and he trod on his bag again. "Did you hear him say 'yes'? But the Devil is not very pretty to look at and I shouldn't bother to see him if I were you."

"Oh, I'm not afraid," said the farmer. "What does he really look like?"

"Well, as far as I know, he may well show himself looking like a village schoolmaster."

"Ugh!" grunted the farmer with a start, "I can't stand the sight of village schoolmasters. But, no matter, as long as I know it's the Devil I shan't mind. I'm quite brave – but don't let him come too near me, mind."

"I'll ask my wizard then," said Little Claus, and he trod on his bag and bent down to listen.

"What does he say?" asked the farmer.

"He says: 'Go over to that chest in the corner and you'll find the Devil crouching inside.' But hold the lid firm so that he doesn't slip out."

The farmer went over to the chest, lifted the lid and peeped inside.

"Ugh!" he shrieked and shrank back. "He looks the very image of our village schoolmaster. What a horrid sight!" And then they drank some more wine to get over the shock, and in fact they went on drinking all through the night.

"You know, you'll have to sell me that wizard of yours," said the farmer. "I'll pay you as much as you like – a whole bushel of money, just say the word."

"Oh no!" said Little Claus. "Just think of all the things he can do for me."

"Oh please," begged the farmer, "I simply must have that wizard. I'd give anything in the world for him."

160

"Oh very well then," said Little Claus. "As you've been kind enough to give me a night's lodging, you can have my wizard for a bushel of money, but I insist on full measure."

"Of course," said the farmer, "but see that that chest is taken away. I won't have it in my home one moment longer. He may still be inside," he added with a shudder.

Little Claus gave the farmer his bag with the dry horse-hide and in return received a whole bushel of money, full measure. The farmer also gave him a wheelbarrow to wheel away the money and the chest.

"Goodbye," said Little Claus and off he went, wheeling the barrow with the bushel of money and the chest (with the village schoolmaster inside).

He reached the other side of the forest where there was a deep, swiftly flowing river. A fine new bridge had been built across it and when he was about halfway across, Little Claus said, loud enough for the schoolmaster to hear: "Now what am I to do with this silly old chest? It's no use to

me. I'd better heave it into the river and get rid of it." And he took hold of one end and lifted it up a bit.

"No, stop!" cried the village schoolmaster from inside the chest. "Let me out! Let me out!"

"Ugh!" cried Little Claus, pretending to be scared. "He's still there! I'd better drop it straight into the river and drown him before he gets out."

"Oh no!" pleaded the village schoolmaster. "Let me out and I'll give you a whole bushel of money."

"Well, that's different," said Little Claus, opening the chest and letting out the village schoolmaster. Little Claus pushed the chest into the river and the schoolmaster ran home and came back to give Little Claus another whole bushel of money.

"I seem to have got a pretty good price for that horse of mine," he said to himself when he got home and counted out his two bushels of money. "Big Claus will be none too pleased when he finds out how rich I've grown from my one horse."

Soon after this he sent a boy over to Big Claus to borrow a bushel measure. "What on earth can he want that for?" wondered Big Claus, and he stuck a bit of tar at the bottom of it so that whatever Little Claus was measuring would stick to it. And indeed that is just what did happen. For when the measure was returned to Big Claus there were two gleaming silver florins sticking to it.

"What does this mean?" said Big Claus and he dashed straight off to Little Claus and asked, "Where have you got all this money from?"

"Oh, that's from the horse-hide which I sold yesterday."

"And a handsome price you must have got for it," said Big Claus. And he hurried back home, took an axe and struck all his four horses down dead. Then he stripped their skins off and drove off to town with them.

"Skins, horses' skins! Who'll buy my skins?" he shouted as he went through the streets. All the tanners and shoemakers

164

came out and asked what price he was asking.

"A bushel of money per piece," he replied.

"A bushel of money!" they all cried in amazement. "Are you mad? D'you think we are fools?" And they took their straps and leather aprons and began to beat him and thrash him until he was chased right out of town. When he got back home that night he was very angry. "Little Claus will pay for this," he kept muttering. "He'll pay with his life for this. I'll kill him."

Just about this time Little Claus's grandmother died. It's true she hadn't been very kind to him (at times she had even been quite nasty), but he felt very sorry all the same and so he took the dead lady over into his own warm bed to see if he could bring her back to life again. He left her there all night and he went and slept in a chair in a corner of the room.

In the middle of the night the door opened and in crept Big Claus with his axe. He made straight for the bed and hit the dead grandmother on the head, thinking it was Little Claus.

"Well, that's finished him," he muttered to himself, "he won't make a fool of me again." And he went off home.

"Well, well," said Little Claus. "What a nasty, wicked man. He meant that blow with the axe for me. It's a good thing old grandmother was dead already or he'd have well and truly done the job himself."

He dressed his grandmother in her Sunday best, borrowed a horse and cart from a neighbour and propped the old lady up on the back seat so that she wouldn't slump out if he drove too fast. Then he started out through the forest. He reached an inn just about sunrise and went inside to have a bite of something to eat.

Mine host the innkeeper was a very rich and very pleasant man on the whole, but there were times when he could get very peppery and lose his temper completely.

"Good morning," he said to Little Claus. "I see you're out early today, and in your best clothes too."

"Yes," said Little Claus, "I'm off to town with my grandmother. She's sitting out there in the back seat of the cart. She won't come in, so would you kindly take her out a glass of mead. And speak up loud, won't you, as her hearing is not all that good."

The innkeeper went out to her. "Here's a glass of mead from your grandson, madam," he said.

The dead lady said never a word and sat quite still.

"Can't you hear?" shouted the innkeeper at the top of his voice. "Here's a glass of mead from your grandson!" He shouted the same thing again and again and as she didn't stir he flew into a rage, completely lost his temper and threw the glass right in the dead lady's face. The mead ran down all over her cheeks and nose and she slumped over the side of the cart – for Little Claus had only propped her up and not tied her fast.

"Now look what you've done!" shouted Little Claus, rushing out of the inn. "You've killed my poor grandmother. Just look at that great cut in her forehead."

"Oh, what a misfortune!" cried the innkeeper, wringing his hands. "It's all because of my hot temper. Dear Little Claus! I'll give you a whole bushel of money and have her buried as though she were my own grandmother. Only don't tell anyone, of course, or they'll cut my head off and that wouldn't be at all nice."

And so Little Claus got another bushel of money and the innkeeper buried the old grandmother as if she had been his own.

Then little Claus went back home and sent a boy over to Big Claus to ask if he could borrow a bushel measure.

"My goodness, what can that mean?" wondered Big Claus. "I killed him, didn't I? I'd better go and see for myself." So off he went to Little Claus with the bushel measure.

When he saw all the money he gaped with surprise. "Where did all this come from?" he asked.

"You didn't kill me," said Little Claus. "It was my grandmother you killed with your axe. And I've sold her for a bushel of money."

"My goodness, that's a pretty good price you've got for her," said Big Claus, and he hurried straight home and killed his grandmother with his axe. Then he put her in a cart and drove to the chemist's and asked him if he wanted to buy a dead body.

"Whose?" asked the chemist. "And where did you get it?"

"It's my grandmother," replied Big Claus. "I've killed her and I'm asking a bushel of money for her."

"Heavens above!" cried the chemist. "What next, I wonder! You must be raving mad. If you go about saying things like that, you'll lose your own head. You're a very wicked man and you deserve to be punished!"

Big Claus got so frightened at this that he rushed out of the shop, jumped into his cart and galloped his horse straight back to his house. The chemist really thought he must have gone mad – and so did everyone

else – and they let him drive wherever he
wanted to.

Big Claus really was mad – with rage.
"You'll pay for this, Little Claus," he kept
saying. "You'll most surely pay for this." And
as soon as he was back home, he took the
biggest sack he could find and went over
to Little Claus and said: "So you've fooled
me again, have you? First, you made me kill
my horses and now my grandmother. But
you are never going to fool me again!" So
saying, he seized Little Claus by the scruff
of the neck, put him into the sack and slung
the sack over his shoulder. "And now, Little
Claus, I'm going to drown you," he said.

Little Claus was no lightweight and Big
Claus had a long way to go before he got
to the river. Along the road they passed a
church where they could hear people singing
hymns to the accompaniment of a beautiful
organ. "It would be rather nice if I went in
and sang a hymn before I go any further,"
thought Big Claus, and so he put down his
heavy burden and went into the church. "Oh
dear! Oh dear!" Little Claus kept saying as

he twisted and turned in the sack; but he couldn't untie the cord. At that moment an old cattle drover was passing, with a big stick in his hand and driving a herd of cows and bullocks. One or two of them stumbled against the sack and knocked it over.

"Oh dear!" sighed Little Claus. "I'm so very young and I'm going to heaven already."

"And I'm so very old," said the drover, "and I can't get there yet!"

"Open the sack," cried Little Claus. "Change places with me and you'll go to heaven straight away!"

"Gladly will I do that," said the old drover, and he undid the sack and out jumped Little Claus.

"You *will* look after my cattle," said the drover, getting into the sack.

"To be sure, I will," said Little Claus, and he tied up the sack and then went off with the cows and bullocks.

Soon Big Claus came out of the church and flung the sack over his shoulder, thinking how light it had become – the old drover was less than half the weight of Little Claus. "He's grown light as a feather," he muttered to himself. "It must be the effect of that nice hymn I have sung." Then he made for the river which was deep and wide, and threw in the sack with the old drover inside.

"Take that, Little Claus," he shouted, "you'll not fool me any more."

He then set off home, but at the crossroads whom should he meet but Little Claus himself, driving his herd of cows and bullocks.

"What does this mean?" asked Big Claus, "Didn't I just throw you into the river?"

"Yes, you did," said Little Claus.

"Then where have you got all this cattle from?"

"It's sea-cattle," said Little Claus. "I'm very grateful to you for throwing me in, but let me tell you the whole story. I was really terribly frightened when I was tied up inside that sack, and how the wind did howl when you threw me down from the bridge. I went straight to the bottom, of course, only I didn't get hurt because I fell on to the softest of soft grass that grows on the river bed. And then the sack opened and the loveliest of lovely girls in a snow-white dress, and with a white garland round her hair, came and took me by the hand and said: 'Is that you, Little Claus? Here's some cattle for you, and a mile further along there's another herd for you.' I then saw that the river was a wide sea-road for the sea-people. They were walking along down at the bottom, making their way up to the country where the sea ends. I can't tell you how pleasant it was down there, with flowers and green grass, and fishes darting past like birds in the air. And cattle, too, walking along the dykes and ditches."

"Then whatever made you come up again so soon?" asked Big Claus. "I would have stayed down much longer, as it seems so very nice down there."

"Well," replied Little Claus. "Listen to me, this will just show you how clever I am. You remember I told you the sea-girl said there was another herd of cattle waiting for me. Well, I know the river winds and bends all over the place so I have decided to make a short cut by coming up on land and then diving down into the river again. I'll save almost half a mile like that, and I'll get the rest of my cattle all the quicker."

"I must say, you *are* a lucky man," said Big Claus. "Do you think I could get some sea-cattle if I went down to the bottom of the river?"

"I don't see why you shouldn't," replied Little Claus. "But don't ask me to carry you to the river in a sack, you are far too heavy for me. If you care to walk there and then get into the sack, I'll throw you in with the greatest of pleasure."

"Thank you very much," said Big Claus, "but if I don't get any sea-cattle when I get down there, you can look out! I'll give you the thrashing of your life!"

"Oh please don't be too hard on me," said Little Claus, and off they went across to the river. When the cattle saw the water they ran towards it as fast as ever they could, for they were very thirsty.

"You can see how eager they are to get to the bottom again," said Little Claus.

"Yes, yes," said Big Claus impatiently. "I can see that, but you've got to help me to get in first or else you'll get that thrashing I promised you."

"Very well," said Little Claus, helping Big Claus to get into the sack. "And put a stone in it in case I don't sink," added Big Claus as his head disappeared inside the sack.

"You'll sink all right," said Little Claus. And putting in a large stone, he tied the cord tight and pushed the sack into the flowing water.

"I'm very much afraid he won't get those cattle," said Little Claus, and he drove off back home with what he had got.

The Macaronies Who Went for a Walk

Miloš Macourek
Translated by Marie Burg

To live in a box and never see a thing – that must be an awful bore. There they were, lying in a box in the larder, bored stiff: about one hundred and twenty sticks of macaroni. They were Italian macaronies, so they spoke to each other in Italian.

"What a bore," they said, "what a bore."

"It's so boring," said one macaroni, "we're bored to the teeth – in fact, we could end up eating one another."

"Well, we can't eat one another raw," said macaroni number three. "But why don't we go somewhere? The world is so interesting, after all. It has merry-go-rounds and swings and all sorts of concerts, fancy restaurants, zoos, and goodness knows what else."

"All right," said macaroni number nine, "but will they let us go? People will see us and they'll say, 'Ah! Macaronies!' and they'll grab hold of us, and that'll be the end of our walk."

"We mustn't be recognized," said macaroni number thirty-seven, "so let's wear hats and raincoats."

So they put on hats and raincoats and off they went. They walked the streets, all one hundred and twenty of them, and people said, "Look! Some sort of guided tour."

From time to time the macaronies stopped people who were passing by and asked in Italian, "Excuse us, do you know any interesting sights around here?"

"The trouble is," people said, "we don't know any Italian, but if you want to see something interesting, we've got a merry-go-round and swings, all sorts of concerts, a fancy restaurant, a zoo, and goodness knows what else."

"Well, perhaps we'll try the merry-go-round and the swings first, and then a concert and the zoo," said the macaronies.

"Well, in that case you go such and such a way," people said, and the macaronies walked on and visited the merry-go-round and swings, and a concert, and the zoo.

It was all very interesting, but in the end the macaronies felt cold, their feet were frozen, and they said to one another, "It was all very interesting. All macaronies ought to see things like that. But now let's go and sit down in a restaurant."

So they went into a restaurant, sat down quietly, and chatted together in Italian. When the waiter heard them, he said to himself, "I know how to please them – I'll bring them Italian macaroni. They'll enjoy that!" And that's just what he did – he brought them macaroni.

As you can imagine, it was a pleasant

surprise for the macaronies – the ones sitting at the table as well as the ones lying on the plates – and they all said at once, "What a coincidence! What are you doing here?"

"Well," said the macaronies sitting on the chairs, "we were bored stiff, so we went for a little walk and, because our feet were hurting us, we stopped off here."

"Why didn't we think of that before now?" said the macaronies on the plates to one another. "We might have seen something ourselves."

"It's never too late. We've already seen all sorts of things. But you haven't seen any. Let's change places – you take our hats and raincoats, and we'll lie down on the plates. It's quite simple. Let's get on with it!"

So the macaronies that were lying on the plates jumped down on to the carpet. But the head waiter came running up and said to the ones at the table, "Excuse me, I don't know any Italian, but what sort of manners have you got? All the macaroni is on the carpet, I thought you knew how to eat macaroni."

And he hurried away to fetch a dustpan and brush.

"Here are the hats and the raincoats," said the first group of macaronies to the second. "Get dressed while we get on to the plates." And they climbed on to the plates, dipped their feet in the hot sauce, and felt fine.

When the head waiter arrived with the dustpan and brush, he saw that there were no macaronies on the carpet and that the guests were leaving. He was very surprised. "Why are you leaving?" he wanted to know. "Didn't you like the macaroni?"

"Excuse us," said the macaronies who were about to leave, "but how could we eat macaroni? Since when is genuine Italian macaroni eaten raw?"

The head waiter looked, and he saw that the macaronies on the plates really were raw. He made his apologies, thinking, "What a disgrace!"

But the macaronies wearing hats and raincoats smiled and said, "Never mind, that can easily happen."

And they waved goodbye to the raw macaronies, and went out to have a look at the swings and the merry-go-rounds and at the whole world that is so very interesting.

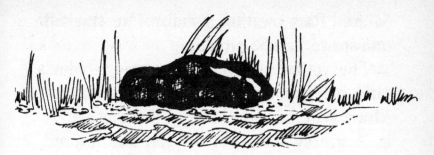

Matt and the Giant Slug

Fay Sampson

"Does it have to be that big?" Matt asked his mum.

"Yes," she said, flinging another spadeful of earth over her shoulder. "It needs a hole in one place a metre deep. So the fish can go there when it freezes in the winter."

"Wouldn't fifty centimetres do? We never get ice that thick." Matt dodged a shower of pebbles and lumps of yellow clay.

"That's what it says in my book," panted

Mum. "Pass me that pickaxe. I've cracked one spade handle already."

The yellow clay had given way to blue. "It's halfway to being rock down here," Mum grunted. She swung the pickaxe at it. A greasy slab split off and she levered it up. Matt sat down on a tree stump and watched. The new pond was going to be an interesting shape. Kidney-shaped, Mum called it. Matt wasn't keen on kidneys. He decided it was more like a sausage that had curled up in the pan and split both ends.

"When's dinner?" he asked.

"If you wanted to make yourself useful, you could shovel that earth into the wheelbarrow and tip it out in the corner. We need to level the terrace."

Matt went on sitting still for a few moments, to make it clear that he hadn't wanted to be useful. Then he got up quite slowly and wandered over to the pile of earth and stones. Mum was still chucking subsoil out of the hole. He waited for a quiet spell, while she was wrestling with a small boulder, put half a dozen quick spadefuls into the barrow, and ran out of the firing-line. He meant to tip it where she wanted it, to make a nice flat patio. But aiming a wheelbarrow exactly is not easy. Half of it tumbled down on to the lawn below the rockery wall.

"All right," said Mum, pushing back her chair with an earthy hand. "I get the message. Dinnertime."

It was late in the afternoon when next she climbed out of the deep hole where the fish could take cover, on to the wide halfway level where she was planning to stack a pile of boulders for an island, up to the narrow ledge for plants around the sides, and on to the bare flat top that would be covered with crazy paving to make a patio.

She smiled broadly. "Not bad, though I say it myself. I think that should do."

"You don't mean you've finished at last, do you?" asked Matt in amazement. "Not *finally* finished!" She had been at it every weekend for months.

"Finished digging. There's a lot more to do yet."

Next week, a lorry arrived and tipped a

load of sand inside the gate. Matt discovered that barrowing sand into the pond-hole was a lot more fun than carting earth away from it. Most of it went in the right place. Mum spread the sand evenly over all the levels and packed it against the sides.

"So any sharp stones I've missed can't stick through and cut a hole in the pond-liner."

Matt went with her to the garden-centre to buy the liner. It was a grey rubbery plastic sheet and cost a lot of money.

"Did you have to make such a big pond?" he asked.

"The country used to be full of ponds once. Then tidy people put in pipes and drained them all away. It's time we put some proper ones back so the things that used to live in water can have homes again."

"Like crocodiles?"

"It's been millions of years since there were crocodiles in Britain."

"Or a brontosaurus? Mr Symonds says they were so heavy they used to stand around in water so it would hold their tummies up."

"I actually fancied frogs myself. But you never know."

"This is the good bit," said Mum when they got home. "I've been looking forward to this ever since I dug the first spadeful."

They spread the plastic liner right over the hole, like a tablecloth. The edges had to be anchored firmly.

"So it won't all slide into the hole when we turn on the tap."

"We can use the stones left over from the rockery," Matt suggested, and ran to get some. Even he was beginning to get excited now. They spaced the stones around all four sides. The liner lay stretched between them, hiding the hole. It sagged a little towards the middle.

"Are you sure it's big enough?" asked Matt doubtfully. "You said that hole was a metre deep. It won't reach to the bottom, will it?"

"It'll stretch," said Mum. "I hope. Here goes!"

She handed one end of the yellow hosepipe to Matt, and took the other end into the kitchen. For a while she fiddled about with screws and clips. Then,

"Stand by for firing."

"Roger."

There was a trickle of water, then a sudden whoosh that nearly shot the hosepipe out of Matt's hands. Then it settled down into a steady flow. Mum came and stood with her hands on her hips, looking pleased with herself.

"Fantastic!"

"It's hardly Lake Michigan yet," Matt pointed out. "More like a birdbath."

"It'll come. This is what I've been waiting for. Just sitting on this tree-stump watching it fill up."

The afternoon passed slowly and peacefully. The water widened. The liner sank lower and lower under the weight. Matt sat down too. He didn't really need to hold the hosepipe. He laid it on the edge and let it pour over all by itself.

After about an hour, he said, "It's working. You can see the shape of your pool coming."

The liner draped itself over the lip of the deepest hole and flattened out across the middle level. Soon after that it touched bottom. The water began to creep higher up the sides. It took a long time. Matt went indoors to watch television.

"Tea?" he said hopefully, when the children's programmes had finished. Mum didn't seem to have heard. He sighed. "OK. I'll get it."

The end of the hosepipe which Mum had screwed to the tap was squirting fine jets of water all over the kitchen. Matt stepped carefully over the slippery floor and found a tin-opener.

When he carried the plates outside, the water was getting close to the top of the pool. They ate baked beans and toast while they watched the last slow centimetres fill.

"It's a bit wrinkly round the corners, isn't it?" Matt suggested.

"A few water-lilies and a clump of bulrushes, and you'll never notice."

Mum scooped up the last of the bean juice on her finger.

"Lovely. I think, I really think, that's it."

She walked dreamily into the kitchen and turned the tap off. The hosepipe coughed and died. Mum came out and stood looking down at the brimming pool, not saying anything. Matt put his arm round her waist and hugged her.

"It's almost a lake, isn't it? I don't know anyone else who's got a pond this big."

After that, every time Matt came home from school, the pond seemed to have sprouted something new. One day there were three fleshy water- lilies, that would have red, pink and yellow flowers before long. Another time there were tufts of reeds, striped green and white. Mum added water-crowsfoot and water-forget-me-not and even water- primroses. The most important plants were the dark green curly Canadian pondweed, sunk underwater.

"To make oxygen for the fish and things," explained Mum.

"What things?" Matt wanted to know again. "Besides frogs. If I'm sharing the garden with something, I'd like to be told."

Mum shrugged her shoulders. "We'll have to wait and see. Let's start with the fish. The water's had time to settle and the plants have got going."

They bought six goldfish.

"You've been robbed," said Matt. "Call them gold? That one's nearly all black."

"They'll change colour as they grow," said Mum hopefully. "No! Don't drop them in! It's not the Olympic diving finals."

Matt lowered the polythene bag into the pool as gently as he could and let the fish swim out. They promptly bolted to the bottom of the deep hole and hid under the stones Mum had put there. Matt didn't see them again for a week.

"They'll be happier when the water gets a bit muckier," said Mum. "It's a bit public when it's so new and clean."

Matt dipped his dirty hands into the water and sloshed them round. A trail of brown water followed them.

"I could have my bath in it."

"I don't think they'd like the soap."

"Your pond's got knobs on," Matt said, feeling the sides of the liner.

"Same to you."

"No, really."

Mum knelt down and looked. "That's a bit of luck. I forgot to buy any pond snails to keep the water clean. And now we've hundreds of baby ones. Look, they're all round the walls. They must have hitchhiked here on the water-plants. This week's special bonus."

"I thought fish didn't want the water clean."

"There's mud and there's sludge. The snails will eat all the rotten stuff."

"Yuk."

The dragonflies came when the waterlilies opened. Shimmering blue and green, they hovered over the water like helicopters.

One night, Matt lay awake hearing a monotonous rattle that came again and again. At last he padded downstairs. Mum was sitting in front of the television with a can of beer.

"I can't get to sleep. There's something creaking in my bedroom. I don't like it."

"I can't afford a new bed for you," Mum said. "It was either that or the pond."

"When I was born, you should have asked the hospital to swop me for a guppy."

"True. It would have been cheaper to feed."

Mum sat in his bedroom and listened. The creaking was still going on.

"It's outside," said Mum. "Put your dressing-gown on and we'll go and have a look."

They went very softly out of the back door. The light from the kitchen fell across the patio.

"Sh!" said Mum, going very quietly to the water's edge. "There!"

A brown warty head was jutting up between two clumps of reeds. Two round eyes bulged. The throat swelled out and collapsed and swelled again. Each time a dry croak rattled from it.

"A frog!" whispered Matt.

"Toad," corrected Mum. "Frogs are green and smooth."

Next morning there were newts.

"I'd no idea there were so many homeless amphibians looking for a pad," Mum said. "I wonder what'll be next."

"You said there was a world pond shortage, didn't you?"

Matt watched the little brown newts crawling slowly over the ledges like underwater dragons. One of them climbed a lobelia stem with tiny clever hands and put its head out of the water. Matt made a grab for it, but the newt dived with an astonishing burst of speed, leaving only ripples spreading from the splash. There wasn't a newt left in sight, or a goldfish either. Matt plunged his hands down into the pondweed. He couldn't feel anything alive.

"It's not a swimming bath," said Mum. "You'll be taking a header soon."

Matt drew his dripping arms out of the pond and sat up. The water trickled down to his elbows.

"It's getting muddier," he said.

There was a streak of brown on his arm. He tried to brush it away. It seemed to be stuck. When he picked at it, he found it was a long thin strip of something soft and squirmy.

"Your pond's got worms," he complained.

Mum inspected it. "That's a leech."

"A leech!" Matt yelled. "They suck blood, don't they? Get it off!"

Mum tugged. The leech came away, leaving a small red mark. "It's only a little one. And it hadn't got a hold. The sort doctors used to use were much bigger than that."

"Shut up," said Matt. "I'd rather not talk about it, if you don't mind. I think I'm going to throw up."

After that, he didn't go quite so close to the edge, or trail his hands in the water.

It was about a week later when he saw it. He was sitting on his favourite tree-stump, watching the dragonflies keeping aerial surveillance over the red waterlily, and trying to spot the toad camouflaged among the floating leaves. Gradually, out of the corner of his eye, he became aware of a darker shadow under an overhanging stone at the lip of the pond where the water level had dropped a few centimetres. At first he thought it was a long wet leaf stuck to the liner. Next time he looked he saw it was too fat and slippery. When he looked again, it had begun to move.

One end had disappeared into a damp hollow under the stone. The rest was slowly sliding after it. It had no legs or wings or shell, and it was a bloated, slimy grey, mottled with black. This was something far bigger than the little threadlike leeches. It was the longest, fattest slug he had ever seen.

When it had poured itself into the darkness, Matt sat there feeling a bit sick. He wished he hadn't seen it. He couldn't get the thought of it out of his mind. It was so horrible that he didn't even want to tell Mum about it.

That night he dreamed.

He was standing outside a beautiful great house, well, a castle, really. There was candlelight inside, and dancing and feasting. Everybody was having a wonderful time. Matt was the owner of the castle. He walked out into the evening and through his wonderful garden. There were statues, and flights of stone steps, and flower-beds full of roses and that sort of thing. He walked down and down, over soft green lawns and leafy paths, till he came to an ornamental lake.

There was a low stone wall around it, and an old boathouse with a punt. He walked up to the wall and stood looking over. The lake was overgrown. Great fields of waterlilies covered the surface. The water between them was green and dark. He peered down. Something swam by under the shadowing leaves. It was the size of a crocodile. It had huge eyes glowing orange like foglamps, and a jagged crest like a torn tin-can, and hundreds of thin curved teeth, like cats' claws. It looked uglier and older than any fish he had ever seen a picture of. He watched it disappear. When he looked round, there was another.

Matt sat up in bed. He was trembling

with fright. Outside he heard the friendly croaking of the toad in the pond.

Next morning, Matt went outside very cautiously. The pond looked all right. Mum was right. The fish were definitely turning gold all over now. He made himself look straight at the hollow under the stone. It was OK. The big slug had gone.

He was just turning away in relief when he saw it. It had crawled to the other side of the pool. It clung there in full daylight, pale and soft. It had horns and eyes.

"Mum," he said accusingly. "There's something nasty in your pond."

She came out and looked at it. "It isn't exactly pretty, but it's harmless. It's only a slug."

"Only! It's ten times bigger than the biggest slug I've ever seen in my life. What does a slug want to be that big for? It's gross."

"Perhaps it's the water," said Mum. "Perhaps it's drunk too much and filled itself up like a water-bed."

"Don't be daft," said Matt. "Its skin

wouldn't stretch that far. Not if it was a normal slug."

"The pond-liner did."

"Aren't you going to get rid of it?"

"No," said Mum. "It's all part of nature's rich variety, poor thing. Toads, newts, slugs. We keep open house here."

Matt dreamed again.

It was night. The moon was casting black shadows over a rough meadow. Matt was a knight riding across country on a lonely quest. Through the trees he saw white mist smoking up over the grass. As he rode nearer he glimpsed water through the fog. He stopped his horse at the brink and dismounted. He was on the edge of a vast silent pool. The farther shore disappeared into the darkness. The water was black and still. No plants grew in it. He listened for the plop of a feeding fish, but there was no sound.

Then a shiver of silver caught his eye. Something was rising from the middle of the pool. Something with a huge horned head and flaring nostrils. Something with great clawed feet starting to wade towards him. Something with a long humped back and a scaly tail. Sir Matt seized his lance and levelled it at the monster. He hurled it with all his strength, but the point glanced off its scales as the beast came lumbering up the shore.

This time Matt's yell woke Mum.

"You'd better stop having cheese for supper," she told him.

"It's that slug," he said hotly. "I told you. It's a giant slug. What if it's only a *baby* giant slug? Think about it."

"No. *Don't* think about it," said Mum. "You've been playing too many computer games."

"What good do slugs do, anyway?" he asked at breakfast.

"We. . .ell. I don't know that they actually do any good. And they do eat lettuces and things."

"Then kill it."

"It hasn't done me any harm. I don't fancy poisoning things with slug-bait. Anyway, our toad might eat it by mistake. I have heard

of people who put out saucers of beer for them to drown in. I tried it once. All I got was a sozzled hedgehog staggering round in circles. It won't hurt you."

"I'm not so sure."

For three more days Matt didn't see the giant slug. But that didn't stop him dreaming about it. He dreamed . . . That was the trouble. He dreamed he couldn't see it. But he knew it was there, in the dark, waiting to get him.

"It's no good," Matt said to himself. "It's either me or him. That slug's got to go."

Mum was upstairs, making the beds. It was a waste of breath asking her to help. She wouldn't believe he was serious. He would have to do it himself.

The slug was back. It was draped across the wet side of the pool between the edge of the patio and the water surface. It looked even bigger than he remembered. It must be at least twenty centimetres long. If he put a stick under it, could he lift it? Or would it squirm and flop on to the paving stones at his feet?

202

Matt knew what he ought to do. He knew what his mum would say. He should pick up the slug on the end of a stick, carry it as far away as possible, and drop it into the bushes to crawl away.

On the other hand . . .

Matt picked up the biggest stone he could find. With both hands he swung it high over his head. Once more he looked down at the fat slug at his feet, and . . .

"Matt! Whatever are you doing?" Mum was hanging out of the bedroom window.

Matt jumped with guilt, and dropped the stone. It fell into the pond with an enormous splash. All the goldfish disappeared.

"I . . . er . . . I was . . . um . . . practising weight-lifting."

"No, you weren't," said Mum. "You were going to squash that poor little slug, weren't you?"

"Poor little . . . !" gasped Matt.

Next minute, Mum was beside him on the patio.

"Look! Poor old sausage! You've terrified the daylights out of it."

Matt turned round. The slug was no longer sprawled wetly across the plastic pool-liner. It had bunched itself into a hard loop, hardly half the size it had been. If it could have galloped for safety, it would. It was humping itself towards its dark hidey-hole as fast as it could.

"Well, I suppose it's not really *gi-normously* big," said Matt doubtfully. "And it hasn't got teeth."

"Oh, yes, it has," said Mum. "But not big enough to eat you. They're on its tongue."

"On its *tongue*! You're making this up."

"Would I do a thing like that? It shoots it out and wraps it round things, like an elephant's trunk does."

She lifted a juicy, green leaf on its wet stalk. A bite had been taken out of it. The curve looked smooth, but when Matt peered very closely he could just see a zigzag edge.

"Crumbs!" said Matt. "It's like a circular saw."

He sat down on the patio for a think. Unfortunately, it was just where the splash from his stone had landed most of the water. Matt got up and moved very softly to stand over where the slug had disappeared. The edge of the paving-slab overhung the pool. Presently, Matt picked another leaf. He lowered himself on to the warm stone and moved his leaf carefully in front of the hole. If he sat very quietly and waited very patiently, he might, he just might, mightn't he, see a pair of little horns with knobs on, and a tiny tongue shoot out, covered in teeth?

One is One and All Alone

Nicholas Fisk

Dear Diary,

I get so lonely, that's my trouble. I am the only child on this ship. Everyone else is a grown-up, with things to do. They're all busy running the ship or checking their equipment for when we land on Trion.

Yes, we're heading for Trion! Isn't that exciting? No, it's not. Not exciting at all.

When we set out I used to tick off the days on my calendar. We left Earth on 12 March 2045. So I ticked off March 12, 13,

14, 15 ... Then April ... May ... June.
Then I gave up. We don't reach Trion until
mid-January 2047. By then I'll be eleven.
Eleven! Isn't that exciting? No, it's not.
I'll still be the same old Trish, but bigger
and older.

Dad does his best, he's always poking
his head round the door, grinning at me.
"How's things? Everything all right? How
about you and me meeting in the café at
six for a chocolate whip?"

I grin back and say "Yum, yum!" but even
as I say it his face changes, the grin is still
there but the busy look is back in his eyes:
there are a thousand things in his mind.
After all, he's the ship's Executive Officer,
a big man. Even when he talks to you he's
glancing sideways at the latest printouts.

And I suppose he misses Mum as much
as I do. Almost as much, anyhow. She's
on Trion, helping set up the base and
everything. Busy Dad, busy Mum.

Which leaves me all alone in front of
my Voice-Printer, talking to it, talking and
talking. Then I watch it print out what I've

been saying, my private diary. It corrects my spelling and punctuation. It's clever. I can switch it from Diary to Dialogue – from Graphics to Constructs. For instance, I've taught it to make jungles for me, full of animals leaping about. And it has taught me games and lessons. I suppose it's my best friend, really. Let's switch from Diary to Dialogue and find out . . .

Are you my best friend, VP?

I hope I am, I try to be. But later, on Trion, you will meet human companions: boys and girls like yourself.

Not for a long time, VP.

We must be patient. Meantime, I am your true friend. Shall we play a game? Popstar! Shall we play that?

OK, VP. Do a construct for me, a really good one. Let's have a heavy drum roll, then I make my entrance through clouds of coloured smoke. I'd like a big swinging chain round my neck.

This OK?

Great. Right, here I come, through the smoke ... two, three, four – action!

I begin singing and the other Me, the pop star on VP's enormous screen, acts out being a pop star. VP has made me taller and older, about seventeen. VP is terrific on Constructs.

Exciting, isn't it! No, it's not.

I'm sick of Me, sick of being the ship's Only Child, sick of computer images and sounds. If only I had someone to talk to, to be with! Someone of my age ...

You know what I mean, don't you, VP?

Of course I do. I sympathize. Shall we play something else?

No, let's not play any more. Teach me something. Where did we get to last lesson?

We reached 'Clo'. So I taught you about clocks.

What follows clocks?

Clone. C-l-o-n-e. Clones and cloning.

Teach me about clones and cloning, then.

Certainly. A clone is the exact reproduction of a living thing made by taking a small part of the original – a scrap of tissue, say – and using this scrap as the pattern from which a duplicate of the original is created.

Oh dear!. . .No, wait, I remember now. They cloned frogs in the last century, didn't they?

Frogs and many other animals.

That's right – they took a tiny scraping from the frog's skin and sort of brewed up hundreds of frogs from that little scraping?

Quite so. And all the frogs were identical because all were constructed from the same original to the same pattern.

210

I bet it was complicated!

It was. It is.

You mean, it's still done?

Certainly. Why, the resources available in this ship's BioLab would be sufficient to set up a clone laboratory. You see, all that is required . . .

VP went on and on describing cloning techniques. I paid no attention because I was thinking, very hard. But I made sure to record VP's words.

I'll tell you what I was thinking. The BioLab in this ship is very big. It has to be, because biology is what this trip is all about: the biology of Trion – what lives there now, what and who could live there in the future.

At this moment the ship's BioLab is deserted. It won't become busy until we reach Trion.

I need to use it.

I need it all to myself.

I will make a clone. It will be my perfect friend and companion.

211

Perfect, because I am going to clone *myself.* Make another Me.

Dear Diary,

I haven't spoken to you for ages because I've been so busy with my new friend, Clo.

Clo for "Clone".

Clo is me. I am Clo. We are identical twins. No, even closer than that. Clo is made *of* me, *from* me. We are one.

Except that there are two of us! – which is tricky. I mean, suppose Dad put his head round the door and saw two Trishes instead of one!

But I've solved that. My cabin door leads to an identical cabin next door. Clo can vanish through the door like a ghost, in a split second. The next-door cabin is empty, of course – all the cabins are: they won't be filled until the return trip from Trion. So I sleep here, Clo sleeps there. Clothes, food, toothbrushes? Well, yes, I now need two of everything – but the ship is loaded with stores, nobody notices or cares about an extra toothbrush, an extra towel.

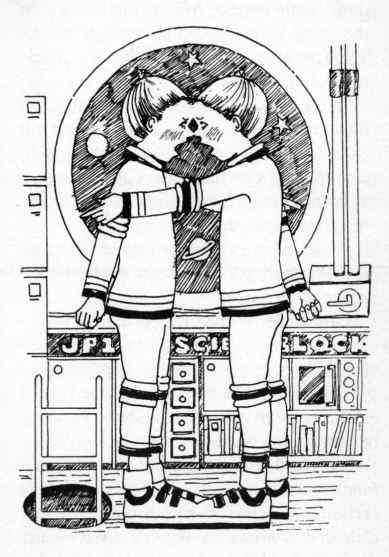

In fact, everything's fine as long as we don't both appear in the same place at the same time! We simply arrange *not* to. Though, just the other night, we nearly made a big mistake. . .

In the middle of the night I had to go to the loo. It's just down the corridor. I got out of bed, opened the door – and met myself, face to face! For there was Clo. We stared at each other, eyes and mouths wide open, then burst into identical giggles.

Which all goes to show how identical we are. We even get the urge to go to the loo at the same time!

No wonder we're such perfect friends.

Dear Diary,

Once again, it's been a long time since I made an entry. There have been so many things on my mind.

The truth is, Clo can be a bit of a pain sometimes. Only in small ways, nothing serious. But this *picking* habit . . . When Clo has nothing to do, it's always pick, pick, pick. Rolling bits of skin around a fingernail. You can't avoid looking at the fingers, they writhe and fiddle all the time. Pick, pick *pick*.

The other evening, I'd had enough. I gave Clo a good old glare and said, loudly and plainly, "Look – do you *mind*? Stop picking at yourself!"

You'll never believe it, but at the very moment I said those words, Clo glared at me and said, "Look – do you *mind*? Stop picking at yourself!"

Me, a picker! I never pick at my fingers. Those tiny little bits of frayed skin – well, they just happen naturally; everyone's got them.

I can't stand people who pick.

Dear Diary,

Long time no see, but here I am again talking to dear old VP, my only true friend.

Clo is in the other cabin, having a sulk-in. It's always sulks these days and they always start the same way . . .

"Don't keep *repeating* me!"

"I wasn't repeating you, I spoke first!"

"You didn't. I did."

"Well, even if I didn't say it first, I *thought* it first. I can't even have my thoughts to myself, you're always butting in and – and – interrupting my train of thought!"

"Interrupting my train of thought!"

So we even use the same words at the same time.

At first it was a joke. We'd catch ourselves doing it and laugh. But I'm not laughing any more, I can tell you. You don't want to share *everything*: some thoughts are private.

Last night Clo did something I cannot forgive. I was thinking about Mum – I'm always thinking of her – and I suppose I gave a sort of sigh and murmured, "Oh, Mum . . ."

As I said it, Clo said exactly and precisely the same thing. "Oh, Mum . . ." Clo said, and gave a sigh.

Now, that's going too far, don't you agree? I mean, my mum is *my* mum, nothing to do with Clo. *My* mum, mine only.

I'm not going to put up with this kind of thing. It's like being swamped, invaded, taken over. You can't even go to Commissary & Stores and pick yourself a pair of new shoes – white shoes with red leather bits, really smart – without finding the *other* person wearing exactly the same shoes.

And crossword puzzles. We don't share the same room, Clo and I, if we can avoid it; so I started doing those old-fashioned crossword puzzles. You do them on your own, with your head down and your mind fully occupied.

Well, how would *you* like it when, after puzzling over a clue for ages, you suddenly find the answer and shout it out – "*NAVIGATOR!*" – and, at that very moment, hear a voice from next door shout "*NAVIGATOR!*"

And those are only the small things. To be truthful, I can't stand the way Clo's mind works. I can't stand Clo's corny jokes, dismal sulks. I can't stand Clo's laugh or eating habits or finger picking. And I *won't* stand Clo intruding on my most private and personal thoughts.

One of the features of this ship is its

disposal system. There are five big hatches, each one marked DISPOSAL. You open the hatch – put the thing you want to get rid of into the hole – and *whoosh*, it's gone. Disposed of for ever into infinite space.

One of the five hatches happens to be just outside my cabin, in the corridor. There's never anyone in the corridor at night.

There you are, then. Tonight's the night. I'll be disposing of something, definitely. I could even write a note to go with the item to be disposed of. The note would read, "Goodbye, Clo. Have a good trip. Yours never, Trish."

Well, it wouldn't be murder, would it? How could it be? You can't be charged with murdering *yourself*, can you? You couldn't even be charged with suicide, because there's still a person left and that person is alive – walking and talking, eating and sleeping.

So it's foolproof. Goodbye, Clo. Yours never, Trish.

Dear Diary,

Over and done with. Finished and forgotten.

No, that's not true! There's no question of *forgetting*. Just the opposite. Every minute of every hour, I mentally hug myself and give a silent shout of "Whoopee! Yarroop! Hooray! Finally free! Alone at last!"

Even Dad noticed. "You're looking wonderful today," he said. "Suddenly you're bright as a button!"

"I feel terrific," I said. "Can I have a chocolate whip?"

"Have as many as you like."

"Just one," I said. "Only *one*." One's enough, isn't it? Who needs two? There's only one Me! No longer do I have to remind another Me to wipe chocolate froth from its greedy mouth. No longer do I have to listen to that other Me's corny "Yum-yum!" noises whenever chocolate whips are mentioned. From now on, there's only one Me. You've no idea how wonderful it feels; how bright the future looks.

Too bad about Trish, of course. "Down

the hatch!" I said. The hatch went *whoosh*. "Goodbye, Trish," I said. "Fond remembrances, I don't think."

But that's something I must remember from now on – my name. It isn't Clo any more. Now I'm Trish.

Trish, that's me.

Acknowledgements

Penguin USA for 'Cheese, Peas and Chocolate Pudding' by Betty van Witsen, from *Believe and Make Believe* ed. Lucy Sprague Mitchell and Irma S Black. Penelope Lively and Octopus Publishing for 'The Great Mushroom Mistake' from *Uninvited Ghosts*, published by William Heinemann Ltd. Naomi Lewis and Victor Gollancz Ltd for 'Vasilissa, Baba Yaga and the Little Doll' from *The Silent Playmate*, published by Victor Gollancz Ltd. Leila Berg for 'The Lory who Longed for Honey' from *The Nightingale and Other Stories* (Oxford University Press), © Leila Berg 1951. Grace Hallworth and Octopus Publishing for 'How Fire Came to Earth' from *A Web of Stories*, published by Methuen Children's Books. Margaret Freaves and J M Dent & Sons Ltd for 'Swing High Swing Low' from *The Lost Ones*, published by J M Dent & Sons Ltd. Margaret Mahy and J M Dent & Sons Ltd. for 'Patrick Comes to School' by Margaret Mahy, from *Chocolate Porridge and Other Stories* (J M Dent, 1987). Michael Rosen for 'The Rajah's Ears', from *The Kingfisher Book of Funny Stories*. Alexander McCall Smith and Canongate Publishing Ltd for 'Strange Animal', from *Children of Wax* (Canongate, 1989). Geoffrey Summerfield and Ward Lock Educational for 'Vardiello', from *Tales Two*. Faber & Faber Ltd for 'Big Claus and Little Claus' translated by Stephen Corrin, from *A Time to Laugh*. Miloš Macourek for 'The Macaronies who went for a Walk' translated by Marie Burg form *Pohádky*, published by Dilia. Fay Sampson for 'Matt and the Giant Slug', © Fay Sampson 1991. Nicholas Fisk and Laura Cecil Literary Agency for 'One is One and All Alone', © Nicholas Fisk 1987, from *Living Fire and Other Science Fiction Stories*, published by Corgi.

The publishers gratefully acknowledge the above for permission to reproduce copyright material. Whilst every effort has been made to trace the appropriate sources for the stories in this collection, in the event of an erroneous credit the publishers will be more than happy to make corrections in any reprint editions.